BEAUTIFULLY ANGELIC

CANDIED CRUSH #2

CHARITY PARKERSON

—Warning: This book is intended for readers over the age of 18.

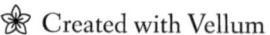

INTRODUCTION

Two men secretly in love. Neither one wants to make a move. It's about to explode in everyone's faces.

Declan has always secretly been in love with Ezra, but it's always been a hopeless love. With Declan working for Ezra's brother, he's not free to show his heart. That hasn't stopped Declan from watching and dreaming about Ezra. Some might even say Declan stalks Ezra on occasion. He can't help it. Ezra is beautiful and sweet. He makes Declan crave everything. But Ezra's brother saved Declan from a horrible life once. Declan can't repay Jessie's kindness by messing with his little brother.

Loving Declan killed Ezra's heart years ago. Declan is amazing and Ezra can't stay away, even though Declan never does anything except hurt him. Each time Ezra thinks they might be close to crossing some invisible line that keeps them apart, Declan shoves Ezra away and sleeps with other people. The pain is something Ezra can't tolerate any longer. His last attempt to win Declan finally pushed him too far. He's done with Declan. Possibly, he's done with everything.

When Ezra's health starts backsliding, Declan must choose. He can stay loyal to the friend who rescued him or save the man he loves. Either way, Declan looks destined to lose someone. Unless love wins the day, that is.

ONE

Shaking permeated Ezra's bones. The Back Porch, Ezra's favorite coffeehouse, was packed with people. Ezra should have been burning up from all the combined body heat, but no. Even in a thick sweatshirt with Sherpa lining, Ezra was freezing. It was as if ice had settled into his soul. Maybe it had. Since Christmas Eve five weeks ago, Ezra felt dead. He just kept moving and smiling despite his non-living status. Hell, he was even serving coffee at The Back Porch to help his friend, Wrecker. If that wasn't trying, Ezra didn't know what was.

Ezra's brother Jessie had gotten married the day after Christmas, stealing away Wrecker's best employee. Even though Jessie had sent Wrecker some temporary help to cover the loss, no one ever

1

worked out. So Ezra would throw himself into things, taking orders and delivering piping hot cups of coffee. He didn't accept tips and refused to let Wrecker pay him. Ezra didn't work here. He just needed to keep moving because he was cold. Ezra wondered if this was how zombies felt. If they were a real thing, that is.

While trying to keep warm, Ezra moved from table to table, checking on Wrecker's customers. At some point, he lost his smile and just kept moving. Ezra couldn't stand still. If he did, he would think about Declan. All roads always led back to Declan. Ezra swallowed a growl. There Declan was again, invading his mind without permission. At fifteen, Ezra's mom had passed. While she had been a wild woman who loved men and life, she had always been an awesome mom. Then she was gone. Ezra found his life uprooted. Living with his bother Jessie might have saved him in some ways during his time of need, but it had also killed him another way—Declan McDaniel.

Declan had been Jessie's bodyguard since shortly after Jessie hit it big when he was a teen. Declan was massive. He took up too much space. Declan was the perfect size to keep Jessie safe from tons of adoring fans. He was also Ezra's biggest secret. Ezra loved him. Always had. It was a love that slowly killed Ezra until he ended up where he was now—cold and alone.

"You have to try this cake I made."

Ezra pulled himself from his depression long enough to focus on Wrecker.

Wrecker was sweet and he cared. Ezra could see Wrecker's concern written in his every feature. Even though he smiled, Wrecker looked tense. It was all Ezra's fault. Ezra couldn't seem to shake the sadness anymore. He had moved beyond the ability to hide it. "Thank you. Maybe I'll take some home with me."

Wrecker's sweet smile slipped away. He snagged Ezra's arm and hauled him in a for a hug. "I wish you would talk to me." Wrecker was huge and warm. He made Ezra wish he could feel anything through the darkness coating his brain.

Ezra snuggled close to Wrecker's chest. His pale hand looked even paler and fragile while resting on Wrecker's dark bicep. Wrecker was the real reason his coffeehouse was always packed. He was muscular and sexy as sin. Gay men flocked the building, looking for any shot with the ex-linebacker. But if Wrecker ever took anyone home, Ezra never saw it. He was content in being a successful businessman. Ezra wished he had that spark for life.

Hell, he wished he cared about anything at all anymore. He just didn't.

"You shouldn't worry so much about me. I've been taking care of myself for a long time now."

"I know," Wrecker said, kissing the top of Ezra's head. "But I know you liked having Theo living with you, and now he's married your brother, and you're having to adjust to an empty house again. I just wish you'd come stay with me or something. Let me take care of you for a while. God knows you're always doing a lot for me."

Ezra patted Wrecker's arm and pulled away. His throat felt tight. His bones were cold. He needed to get moving again. "Seriously. I'm fine."

The deep line between Wrecker's eyebrows said he didn't believe a word leaving Ezra's lips. He picked up the chocolate cake he had been trying to get Ezra to try all night. "Then take one bite of this cake. Don't insult my cooking by refusing."

With a faked smile, Ezra grabbed the fork and scooped up a bite. He forced the food into his mouth by sheer will. His stomach heaved. "Yum," Ezra said around the bite while trying not to choke. It was like ash in his mouth.

"Good. Now I'll pack you the rest to take home. I expect you to finish every bite."

Ezra nodded while praying he wouldn't puke. Wrecker's cake was probably delicious—like everything he cooked—but Ezra's body was currently rejecting all forms on nourishment—like it fought its way to the grave, turning its back on living. The instant Wrecker wasn't looking, Ezra spit the cake into a napkin before he humiliated himself with a round of dry heaves.

No one understood what it was like to be Ezra. Everyone wanted him to be pretty—like he was in the heavily photoshopped magazines he appeared in, but he wasn't. Not really. Not on the inside anyhow. Declan knew that about Ezra. He saw that Ezra was ugly where it mattered most. That was why Declan didn't love Ezra back and never would. That was why Ezra would always feel cold.

THE SCENT OF EXPENSIVE COFFEE PERMEATED the air, coating everything. Declan swore the smell alone nearly overdosed him with caffeine as he stepped through the front door at The Back Porch. Gay men always packed the large coffeehouse. Owned by an ex pro linebacker, The Back Porch served as sort of a haven for men who didn't like the party scene. Declan didn't care about that. Only one thing brought him here... well, one person. Ezra Thunder.

As younger brother to one of the most famous drummers in modern-day history, Ezra didn't need to work. Ezra's brother Jessie paid all Ezra's living expenses. That didn't stop Ezra from pursuing a modeling career, or—for whatever reason—serving coffee at The Back Porch. Declan only knew Ezra had been helping out around here because Declan stalked Ezra. Always. Declan worked as head of security for Ezra's brother. Sometimes that meant taking care of Ezra too. His job had nothing to do with this. In fact, Declan was technically on vacation right now. Everyone thought Declan had been traveling the country the past five weeks. The truth was a lot more sordid.

Declan always took off six weeks at Christmas to throw himself into his biggest sickness—Ezra. Declan followed him. Watched him. Loved him from afar. He knew he was crazy, but this time of year was important. This was the time of year when Ezra almost died eight years ago. Declan hadn't gotten over it. It seemed he had been right to be crazy. Ezra had that same look about him as he had that year. That was the only reason Declan had come out of the shadows over a week ago. He planned to spend what was left of his vacation time openly shadowing Ezra. Ezra could just get the fuck over it.

Declan chose an open table close to where Ezra stood. There was no way he missed Declan's presence. At one time, Ezra might have rushed to Declan's side with a smile and a hug. Now Ezra pretended Declan didn't exist. Goddamn, he looked beautiful. Ezra was a small guy with pink highlights. He couldn't be overlooked. All eyes always followed him. He looked exactly like someone whose face should be plastered all over every magazine. Even Ezra's lips were perfect. They were full and pink, begging for kisses. His hazel eyes were always lit— like Ezra carried an inner light. Those gorgeous eyes never focused on Declan any longer. Declan had been coming to The Back Porch every single night Ezra worked for the past week, and every single night, Ezra pretended Declan wasn't there. Declan had earned Ezra's hatred. He couldn't stop trying to fix it.

At fifteen, Ezra's mom had passed away, leaving Ezra nowhere to call home. Jessie had taken Ezra in and moved from being Ezra's brother to being more like a father. Declan had been twenty-six at the time and possessed zero interest in suddenly finding himself forced to oversee a teenager's safety. He had signed up to tour with a metal band and live the life of a superstar, not babysit a moody teen. Declan had never expected Ezra, though. Ezra had shown up and immediately stolen everyone's hearts. Declan's more than anyone's. For nine years now, Declan had managed to keep a safe distance, being only Ezra's friend. Until Ezra had kissed him on Christmas Eve, that is. Declan had rejected Ezra. Things were fucked between them now, and Declan didn't know how to fix it. All Declan knew was, he had to make them right again.

"Could I get some coffee?" Declan asked when Ezra was within earshot. Ezra kept his head down and kept moving—like Declan was invisible.

Wrecker, the owner of The Back Porch, immediately appeared at the edge of Declan's table, swooping in like he had appointed himself Ezra's protector. "What can I get you?"

Declan swallowed the growl rising in his throat. "A black coffee, please."

Wrecker nodded but didn't move away. Declan found himself staring into Wrecker's oddly colored eyes. They looked like a lion's eyes. Wrecker was a big guy. He matched the image of a pro-level linebacker. Right now, he also looked like he wanted to match his size against Declan. Declan would always win. "Why do you keep coming here? He doesn't want to talk to you."

"I like the coffee."

"You never touch the coffee," Wrecker shot back.

Declan didn't back down either. "Have Ezra bring it to me, and I will."

Some blond guy slid into a chair at Declan's table, looking ready to shoot his shot. Wrecker and Declan focused on the guy. "Get lost," they said simultaneously before going back to staring each other down.

"He doesn't want you here."

Declan shrugged at Wrecker's claim. "Then he can tell me that himself."

Wrecker's features hardened. "I'm telling you for him."

"Oh, for fluff's sake, come on, Declan. We can talk outside," Ezra said, appearing at Wrecker's side.

As thrilled as Declan was to have Ezra's attention, he wasn't quite finished with Wrecker. Wrecker had bucked up to him and Declan couldn't stand for that, especially when it came to Ezra. Ezra belonged to Declan. Always had. Always would. "What about your boss here?" Declan asked, holding Wrecker's stare.

"Wrecker isn't my boss. He's my friend and he's short staffed. I'm just helping where I can. Now do you want to talk or not?"

Judging by the impatience in Ezra's voice, it was now or never. Declan withdrew from his pissing contest and stood. "Let's go." Declan ignored Wrecker's hate-filled stare as he followed Ezra outside. Ezra looked even smaller than usual. His large sweatshirt swallowed him whole. Declan fought the urge to snatch Ezra off his feet and take off running. He could toss Ezra in his truck and take off. Maybe if they had a few weeks alone, Declan could fix them. He didn't know if a few minutes of talking outside would make a damn bit of difference.

"Aren't you supposed to be in Wyoming or someplace like that?" Ezra asked the moment they stepped outside.

"I came back early," Declan lied. He could hardly say he had never left and spent all his time stalking Ezra. "I wanted to see you. Plus, Icarus misses you. He's been a depressed mess since you left him with me without saying goodbye." It was a low blow, but Declan wasn't above such things. Ezra had given him a pit bull puppy for Christmas right before he kissed Declan. Since things had gone badly, Ezra had run for it and not looked back.

Guilt settled into Ezra's features. His eyes slid toward Declan's truck. "Is he with you?"

"No. I didn't want him chewing up the inside of my truck while I came to see you." An evil smile stretched Declan's lips. "So I stopped by your house on the way and dropped him off there before coming here."

For a moment, Ezra blinked as if he couldn't comprehend Declan's words. When he spoke, his words came out slow—like he hoped Declan would stop him before the accusation fully fell. "So you're saying you broke into my house."

There wasn't an ounce of shame in Declan's heart. "It's not breaking in if I know the code to your front door and alarm." Declan didn't give Ezra time to rip into him. "I figure if I don't take you home pretty soon, he'll have time to chew up at least three pairs of your expensive shoes."

"I'll tell Wrecker I'm going."

Declan hadn't expected such a calm acceptance. He didn't trust it. Still, he nodded. "I'll go wait in the truck."

Ezra didn't quite meet Declan's gaze as he nodded and headed back inside. Declan couldn't look away. Damn, he had missed everything about Ezra. No one knew how completely obsessed he was with the man. It wasn't right. Jessie might be Declan's boss, but he was also Declan's best friend. Declan shouldn't want Jessie's little brother this much, but he did.

Declan climbed behind the wheel of his truck to wait. Pretending to go out-of-town while not actually going out-of-town had given Declan some real insight to Ezra's life lately. Ezra had never gone longer than two days without seeing his brother. Since Christmas, as far as Declan could tell, Ezra hadn't been to see his brother at all. They needed to get past this. Declan couldn't let Ezra cut his brother out of his life to ignore Declan's existence. There had to be a middle ground. Declan would find it.

It was taking longer than Declan expected for Ezra to make his way back outside. Declan sat forward and eyed the building. A movement from the corner of his eye caught Declan's attention. He turned his head. Ezra was walking down the road, as if intent on sneaking back home without Declan. With a growl, Declan fired his truck to life. Ezra must have slipped out the coffee shop's back door.

Declan whipped to the side of the road ahead of Ezra and waited. He watched Ezra in the mirror, in case Ezra thought to make a run for it. Instead, Ezra climbed into the passenger seat, looking defeated.

"Were you really trying to sneak away from me?"

Ezra shrugged as he buckled his seat belt. He still didn't look Declan's way. "Does it matter? In the end, you'll always have your way, no matter my feelings."

"Is that truly how you feel?"

Ezra didn't respond.

Declan wanted to punch the steering wheel until his knuckles bled. Ezra made him insane. He didn't know how to make Ezra understand he felt like he was failing everyone, including himself. He loved Ezra. Ezra was who Declan wanted to spend his life with. He just didn't know how to make that happen without taking a sledgehammer to the life he had built, so he did nothing. By doing nothing, he hurt Ezra. It was this horrid and vicious cycle that Declan felt paralyzed to change.

They didn't have far to go since Ezra lived a few streets over from the coffeehouse. Declan was thankful since the silence was thick and bitter. He followed closely on Ezra's heels as they headed inside so Ezra couldn't shut the door in his face.

Icarus ran straight for Ezra. The gray and white pit bull puppy with big blue eyes jumped up and down, trying hard to get into Ezra's arms. Ezra made cooing noises as he took off his shoes and grabbed his mail from the side table by the door.

"I see my mail was brought by at some point." Ezra scooped Icarus from the floor and kissed his head. "You've gotten so big and aren't you such a good boy. It doesn't look like you did anything you shouldn't have while we were gone. Such a good boy." Ezra carried his envelopes, including a flat box, and Icarus to the couch. He sat and cuddled with Icarus while pulling papers from their envelopes.

Declan sat across from him. "You're the only person I know who opens their bills first when they have a package."

Ezra kept his gaze locked on his task, still refusing to look at Declan. "They're not bills. These are letters from my fans that were passed along by my manager. I know what's in the box. It's an early edition of my latest magazine spread. Each letter is always a surprise. I'd rather see them first."

A bitter smile tugged at Declan's lips. "So you plan to read your fan mail until I get frustrated and leave."

Ezra tossed the letters aside. His gaze finally locked onto Declan. The hatred in his eyes made Declan regret wishing for Ezra's attention. "What do you want from me, Declan?"

Declan's throat unexpectedly swelled, making his voice gruff. "I want you to stop being mad at me.

Jessie thinks it's his fault you don't come around anymore. That's guilt he doesn't need right after getting out of rehab."

"I still come around. Plus, how would you know? You've been traveling the country for the past month."

"I still have ears and eyes on Jessie's life. You don't come around like you used to and you know it," Declan shot back. Aggravation swelled in Declan's chest. Ezra looked too skinny. His eyes had dark circles beneath them. He needed his only family, but he wasn't reaching out to Jessie, and that was on Declan. Declan didn't know how to make this stop. "I'll quit, if that's what it takes." The offer burst from Declan without thought. That wasn't what he wanted, but that was how far he would go. "You need Jessie and he needs you." Jessie had finally gone to rehab after decades of hardcore drug use. He was clean and happy, but he needed his brother.

"Fuck you."

Declan blinked. Ezra never, ever cursed. It was a hallmark of his personality. He always used cute words to replace bad words, and it was adorable. Declan was stunned speechless.

When he didn't respond, Ezra gave him a sharp nod. "You heard me. Fuck you." This time, Ezra enunciated each word, leaving no room for doubt that Declan heard him correctly. "You are a sorry-ass mother-fucking bastard. You've spent years, and I do mean literally years, pretending to be my friend." Ezra visibly swallowed and blinked back tears. "The truth is you don't care about me at all. All you care about is your job and your cushy life, driving my brother around and playing the bodyguard. I'm just Jessie's little brother. Some pain in the ass you've had to deal with as part of your job."

Declan couldn't breathe. "That's not true."

"Get out. You have nothing to say to me."

Desperation scratched at Declan's brain and skin. This was the most time he had spent with Ezra in ages, and the thought of leaving was tearing him apart. "No."

Ezra stood, set Icarus aside, and leaned Declan's way. His eyes swam with rage and malice. "Get the *fuck* out of my house. I will not spend another second loving you while you fuck everyone with a pulse. You are *not* my friend. We are nothing. I don't know why you came here tonight, but as I said, you have nothing to say to me." Ezra straightened and headed for the door, as if he intended to leave himself if Declan wouldn't. He made it halfway before throwing out his arm, as if seeking purchase from anything. Declan shot to his feet as Ezra crumpled—like his spirit left his body behind.

Declan raced across the room and fell to his knees. Ezra was out cold, and his pulse was weak. His lips were rapidly turning blue and his skin felt like ice. Declan scooped him into his arms and headed for the door. His heart raced and his breath left him in rapid bursts. Ezra had always been tiny, but he felt like nothing but air in Declan's arms. He was nothing but skin and bones beneath his large sweatshirt. The truth slammed into Declan so hard, his knees nearly buckled. Ezra had relapsed. He was starving himself again, and Declan might have known it if he wasn't such a terrible person.

WAKING UP IN THE ER WAS NEVER FUN, BUT Ezra didn't plan to be there long. He was patiently waiting for his IV bags to empty, and then he would be on his way. That was the strategy Ezra concentrated on while everyone else in his room argued. Theo, Jessie, and Declan stood in a circle, talking about Ezra as if he wasn't there. Jessie had rushed in his room with Theo hot on his heels. He had taken one look at Ezra and then focused his rage on Declan. That fact let Ezra know exactly how angry Jessie was. Jessie had never been good at yelling at Ezra, but he had to let his rage go somewhere. Declan was the person standing closest, so he became Jessie's target.

"Tell me what in the fuck is going on."

Everyone was so loud, yelling incoherently while Ezra's head pounded, but Declan sounded oddly calm. Ezra imagined he had been forced to remain steady during a lot of crazy moments over the years to keep Jessie safe.

Declan was the only one speaking in an even-keeled tone as he tried to calm Jessie's obvious panic. "I came back from my trip early and I stopped by The Back Porch. Ezra was there, helping out Wrecker. Since he had walked there, I offered to give him a ride back home." Ezra rolled his eyes at the lies but kept listening. "At his place, I went in so Ezra could play with Icarus. Once inside, he collapsed. I tried waking him, but I couldn't. His breathing was shallow, so I freaked and brought him here. They're saying he is dehydrated and low on some key vitamins. It's nothing serious. Once they pump him full of what he needs, they'll let him go home."

"Fuck all that," Jessie practically yelled, obviously not reassured. "Is he starving himself again? Is that what happened here? Because he swore to me that all that anorexia bullshit was over before he moved out. He's not fucking going home if he can't keep that promise to me."

Ezra had heard enough. He was tired of being treated like he was invisible. He raised his bed a little higher, reminding everyone he was right here and could hear every word they said. "Do you care to hear my side of things?"

Jessie shoved past Declan. Declan took a seat and crossed his arms over his chest—like he had given up and closed himself off from the room. Ezra was grateful for that. He didn't need any more eyes upon him. Jessie's angry stare was enough.

"Let's hear it, then," Jessie barked.

Ezra's gaze slid Theo's way. Theo was the only one who looked understanding, so Ezra looked at him as he spoke. "I guess I got kind of depressed after Christmas. You two had just gotten married and I didn't want to bug you about it."

"You got married," Declan said, obviously finding a reason to finally lose his patience. "You got married and didn't tell me."

Ezra fought the urge to remind Declan of his earlier boast about having ears and eyes inside Jessie's house even when he was out of town. It didn't seem like he knew all the goings-on after all. Jessie and Theo had secretly gotten married in Ezra's living room. Declan hadn't known that one, so ha.

Jessie waved off Declan's words. "Yeah. Don't get mad. We're doing a big wedding later. I just needed some privacy and time alone with Theo after rehab. We're not talking about me right now." Jessie focused on Ezra. "Go on."

Since he looked calm now, Ezra focused on him. "Starving myself wasn't a purposeful thing. I was happy for you and all. I was just sad for my own reasons." He felt Declan's stare as it settled on him. Ezra didn't want to keep talking, but he did. Declan didn't deserve to know his final rejection had broken Ezra "At first, I just didn't feel like eating because I was depressed. I kept thinking it would pass, but it didn't. Instead, my thoughts just kept getting darker. No one was calling. Not my friends or job offers. So my thoughts kept churning, telling me I'm not good enough. That I'm alone. Then I started wondering if I really am getting fat and if no one cares about me because I'm ugly and unappealing. I don't know how these things grow. It just grew, turning into a vicious cycle. I wasn't hungry, so I didn't eat. My appetite would re-emerge and then my brain would remind me that was why no one called. Then I'd lose my appetite again."

Theo sat on the foot of the bed and rubbed Ezra's leg. "Oh, babe. I'm so sorry I didn't text or call while we were gone. You know I'm not used to having a phone, but that's no excuse."

A hot tear rolled down Ezra's cheek. He swiped it away. "It's not your fault. It's no one's fault. I told you, I'm messed up in the head. That's no one's problem but mine. I need to learn to live with being unwanted. That's not on anyone but me."

Jessie swiped a hand through the air, as if calling an end to Ezra's bullshit. "We deal with this as a family. You're coming home with me until you're fixed again."

Ezra's chest nearly caved at the idea of living under Jessie's roof, watching Declan sneaking men from the house. Another tear sneaked out. "No." The word choked him, but he couldn't back down. "You just got married. It's time to focus on yourself. I'd prefer to do this alone." No witnesses.

Jessie wasn't backing down. "You're not doing this alone. I'm sorry, but no. This is one of those times I can't let you have your way. You've already proven you can't be trusted to be left to your own devices."

"I'll stay with him."

Ezra's eyes fell closed as Declan's voice cut through Jessie's lecture.

Declan's voice grew stronger. "He needs to learn to do better without the pressure of failing you every second of the day. So I'll stay with him at his place. You know you can trust me to watch out for him."

Ezra looked to Theo for help. Theo was the only one in the room who understood why Declan could not come stay under Ezra's roof. He was the only one who knew Ezra was in love with Declan while Declan decidedly did not love him back.

Theo looked helpless as he tried interjecting on Ezra's behalf. "Maybe Ezra should have the final say in this. He won't get better if he's chaffing against the process."

Ezra flashed him a grateful smile. It disappeared the moment Jessie focused on him. He looked unbending.

"Fine. What's it going to be, Ezra? Are you coming back to live with me or is Declan moving in with you for a while?"

"Neither. I'm grown. I can seek counseling all on my own."

Jessie's features hardened in a way that Ezra hadn't seen in a long time and he knew he had lost.

"There isn't an option three for you. You're either coming to live with me or Declan is moving in with you. Either way, you're not going back to being alone. I love you and I won't watch you kill yourself, so I suggest you choose what you can live with before I choose for you."

Ezra's gaze skirted the room, taking in everyone's expressions. Theo looked crestfallen—like he had failed Ezra. Jessie looked unmoving. Ezra saved Declan for last. Declan's expression was completely serene, confusing Ezra. In the end, there was only one option Ezra could live with. At least, under his roof, he didn't think Declan would bring another man home and wave him in Ezra's face.

"Declan can stay with me."

Ezra swore he could feel Jessie's and Declan's combined satisfaction over him falling in line. Theo was the only one who looked devastated on Ezra's behalf. Still, Ezra knew no one on the planet really understood. Ezra loved Declan and Declan only ever destroyed Ezra. This was not the best decision for his health, but Ezra would play along for now. Declan couldn't watch him every second of the day. Ezra would find a way around this. One day, they would all regret interfering.

TWO

The minute they got home; Ezra regretted his decision to let Declan stay. Declan refused to let him walk. Even six months ago, Ezra would have loved being in Declan's arms. After getting carried from the hospital to the car and now from the car to the house, it annoyed him. "I can walk."

Declan didn't as much as glance his way as he easily opened the front door with Ezra held against his chest. "I know you can, but you've lost the privilege until you learn how to act right. I can't trust you're not counting the calories burned walking against the calories you can eat. Plus, you're not wearing any shoes."

Ezra rolled his eyes, but he held on tighter as

Icarus threatened to trip Declan on the way to Ezra's bed.

"When was the last time he was fed?"

Declan met his gaze at the question. He looked angry. "Oh, him you're worried about if he doesn't eat."

Ezra looked away and let it go. No one got it. There was no sense in arguing. Everyone thought they had a right to be angry with him over this. No one considered what it was like living inside his head. They didn't realize it had nothing to do with them at all.

Declan took an audible breath. "I'm sorry. You didn't deserve that. I had Johnny bring some groceries for us and Icarus while we were still at the hospital. I'll fix you both a quick bite before bed."

As much as Ezra hated the thought of putting food in his mouth, he would so Declan would leave him alone. Declan set Ezra on the bed. He tugged and pulled until Ezra was covered in all the blankets.

"Stay put," Declan ordered before heading for the door.

Against his heart, Ezra eyed Declan. He was truly the sexiest man Ezra had ever set eyes on. It wasn't fair. Jessie had always joked that at least one of Declan's parents had been a giant. Ezra believed it. Declan was so tall, he had to duck through every door, and he was built like a brick wall. He looked like a dark Viking. His brown hair was always a shaggy mess while his light green eyes took people's breath. He was the one who should have been a model. Declan was solid muscle and dripped sexiness. Ezra didn't think he could be blamed for wanting him. Everyone did. Ezra wasn't special.

With the familiar sinking feeling in his chest growing by the second, Ezra leaned over and helped Icarus into bed since the dog seemed determined to stay with him. Ezra curled onto his side and cuddled up with the sweet puppy he had given Declan for Christmas. As far as Ezra was concerned, Icarus was just one more example of a time when Ezra had given Declan more than he deserved. Ezra had shown up Christmas Eve night with the puppy in his arms and his heart in his throat, wanting nothing more than to make Declan smile. He had hoped to share the holiday with Declan before Declan left for his yearly six-week car trip around the country. Things had immediately gone wrong. After accidentally discovering Declan kept a stash of every magazine Ezra ever posed for, Ezra had gotten the wrong idea. He had thought that meant Declan felt something for him. After all, Theo had said he believed Declan was in love with Ezra, so Ezra didn't think he was crazy. Apparently, Theo and Ezra were wrong. Ezra had made a fool of himself and kissed Declan. He wished he could claim it was the first time he had been stupid when it came to Declan. Every time he let himself get close to Declan, Declan found a way to make him pay. Usually, he made Ezra pay in the form of watching him bring home another man for the night. One would think that constant mental abuse would be enough to break Ezra from his stupid crush, but no. Ezra still wanted him.

"Don't fall asleep before you eat this."

Ezra rolled and sat up at Declan's order.

Declan eyed the dog on the bed. "I don't want him on the bed."

"It's my bed," Ezra said, letting his tone speak for itself. It was his bed. His house. His rules. "I'm really not hungry." Ezra truly did not want to eat anything.

Declan sat next to Ezra's hip and held out the plate. "Eat this one thing and I'll tell you a secret."

Ezra eyed the sandwich Declan offered. It was white bread and peanut butter. Both things were meant to stick to his bones. "Just one secret? That doesn't sound like a fair trade."

Declan's mouth lifted in one corner. "I'll make it a good one."

It was just like Declan to make Ezra incapable of saying no. "All right." Ezra accepted the sandwich and nibbled the corner. He curled his nose without thought. Ezra hated white bread. It had nothing to do with carbs. It was just like a mouth full of starch. Disgusting.

"Yeah, I know," Declan said, rolling his eyes. "You don't like white bread. Well, guess what? Too bad. You can have wheat bread back when you learn how to make good choices again."

Ezra hadn't been the least bit hungry in ages. Declan's angry tone certainly didn't help matters. Ezra set the sandwich aside and rolled back over. He wasn't purposely being an ass or stubborn. It was hard to swallow food when he was upset. Plus, white bread had always been hard for him. It was a texture thing, which wasn't helped by Declan's attitude. Ezra's throat felt too tight to eat.

Declan blew out a breath. "I thought you wanted to know my secret."

"I don't give a single fluff about your secrets. At one time, I would've killed to hear your every thought. That was before you shut me out and let everyone else in. Now, I couldn't care less."

"Do you know those magazines you saw in my room?"

Ezra didn't answer. Declan would choose the one topic Ezra really wanted to know the story behind, especially since Declan truly owned every single magazine Ezra ever posed for... even the ones Ezra had done in secret.

Declan didn't let Ezra's silence detract him from his point. "More specifically, if you recall, the ones where you posed nude and the lingerie shoots. I had to buy more than one copy because I wore them out staring at you."

Ezra rolled and met Declan's stare. Declan had his attention.

"You probably weighed a good forty to fifty pounds more than you do now, and I couldn't stop looking at you. I've never wanted anyone as much as I want you, and you know it, whether you want to admit it or not. You're mad at me. I get that, but at least attempt to look at things from my point of view. Your brother took me in and saved me from a hopeless, pointless life with abusive parents. Was I supposed to repay his kindness by falling on his little brother like a pervert? Wanting you..." Declan took an unsteady-sounding breath. "Loving you feels like I'm betraying Jessie's trust." A bright and unashamed smile stretched Declan's lips. "That didn't stop me from jacking off to those pictures of you so many times that one of my arms is bigger than the other. You need to regain some weight. Right now. I'm thinking I would break you if I tried touching you the way I want."

A loud snort escaped Ezra to hide the way Declan stole his breath. He couldn't let Declan destroy him right now. Ezra had nothing left to give. "You're so full of yourself. I'm not sick because of you and I won't get well just because you've decided you'll pity-screw me."

Declan's eyes fell closed, as if Ezra made him tired. When he focused on Ezra again, he looked so sad, Ezra's heart twisted. As Ezra looked on, Declan's features hardened. "All right. I've had enough of this. Bitterness doesn't suit you. I get that it's my fault, but that's enough." Without warning, Declan crawled onto the bed, straddled Ezra's body, and kissed him.

In his shock, Ezra didn't immediately respond. Then his heart took control. Declan was the only man Ezra had ever loved or truly wanted. A teenage crush had grown and twisted until Declan was the only body he pictured, no matter how many men he took to bed. Ezra opened his mouth over Declan's bottom lip and sucked. Declan gasped and then took control. His tongue stroked Ezra's. The world disappeared along with Ezra's anger. Declan's kiss was so much better than Ezra ever imagined. It was pure skill and reverence. Ezra's eyes stung. He felt loved.

"I need to take care of you. Please let me take care of you," Declan begged between kisses.

"I don't like white bread."

Ezra felt Declan smile against his lips. "You're so spoiled. I'll bring you the jar of peanut butter and you can eat it with a spoon."

"You can put your dick in it since you're so convinced that I'll break."

Declan buried his face against Ezra's chest and roared with laughter. Ezra stole his chance to run his fingers through Declan's hair. His throat unexpectedly swelled. "You said you love me." The words came out sounding strangled.

Declan's laughter died. His gaze locked on Ezra. "You know I do."

"No. I don't. I don't know that anyone loves me anymore, especially me." Ezra's voice broke on the confession. His eyes burned. He hated himself for his weakness, but Ezra was very tired of himself. Some people loved themselves so naturally and openly. Ezra had to fight to tolerate his reflection every single day. It was exhausting. He didn't want to fight anymore.

By the time Ezra fell asleep, Declan felt like someone had beaten his ass. Unfortunately, the night wasn't over for him yet. This wasn't the first time he had battled this disease with Ezra. At sixteen, Ezra had nearly died from this. Declan refused to let this ugly thing get its claws in Ezra again. Thankfully, Declan still recalled all the ways he had helped Ezra fight last time. He got to work. First, he searched the house, throwing out everything that hindered recovery: the bathroom scales, diet products, and magazines with all the dumb diet tips. Next, he went through Ezra's kitchen and made a note of everything he needed so he could place a delivery order. Finally, he tackled the biggest liars in the house—the mirrors.

With everything finally finished, Declan sank onto the couch. His hands shook. Every time he thought about Ezra collapsing, he wanted to wake Ezra and feed him again. Declan hated this. Even though—logically—he knew eating disorders were forms of mental illness that he had no control over, he felt responsible. He had always known Ezra was more fragile than other people. That hadn't stopped him from pushing Ezra. While he had never purposely risked Ezra's health with his bullshit, he also hadn't kept his distance to spare Ezra. Declan couldn't stay away. That wasn't even an option for him. That meant Declan had to make a choice: Jessie or Ezra. Declan touched his lips. He could still feel Ezra's kiss. There was no turning back from that kiss without completely destroying Ezra, so it seemed his choice had been made while his brain hadn't been working. Fuck. He didn't have the mental spoons to face that tonight. For now, he had to work on healing Ezra and let tomorrow take care of itself.

The flat box from earlier caught his attention. It was on the floor with the corner chewed away. With a groan, Declan went after it. It seemed Ezra had praised Icarus for not chewing up his house a little too soon. As he lifted the box, he realized it was already open, which made sense when he thought about it. Jessie and Ezra were like all the uber rich; they didn't have mailboxes. Instead, their mail was sent to a private office, where it was sorted and then passed along after proper handling and inspection. They only saw what they wanted to see.

Declan carried the box to the couch. He chewed his bottom lip, fighting himself. Declan lost the battle against his curiosity. He opened the flaps and looked inside. His gut twisted as he caught sight of the cover. It was another skin magazine. Jessie would die when he inevitably found out about this. Declan had no such qualms. He needed to see. Declan quickly flipped through the images, uncaring of anyone other than Ezra. His breath caught as the picture of Ezra jumped out at him. His heart skipped a beat as the full image came into view. It was completely tasteful and yet still hot as hell. Ezra wasn't nude, but he might as well have been. He wore a see-through lace thong, heels, and nothing else. Goddamn. He was beautiful. There would be men all over the world drooling over these images and none of them had any clue. Ezra's inner beauty eclipsed any picture he took. No one could look at him and know how completely selfless and kind he was.

Declan put the magazine back in the box. He knew how stunning Ezra was where no one could see, and that had done nothing to change how Declan had been treating him the past few years. Declan wasn't blind to Ezra's feelings. No one on the planet looked at Declan with the heat and love that Ezra did. But they were complicated. Loving Ezra wasn't the easy choice. While Declan knew beyond a shadow of a doubt that he could withstand losing anything and anyone to be with Ezra, he couldn't lose Ezra. Fear paralyzed him at the thought of making his play and ending up alone. Declan had been raised by a mean drunk. Jessie had rescued him from that life. If he chose Ezra, and then Ezra and he didn't work out, Declan would be completely alone in the world. It was a terrifying thought.

Exhaustion washed over Declan. Icarus was asleep with Ezra and Declan didn't want to wake him to take him outside before bed, so Declan spread out some puppy pads and hoped for the best. He checked on Ezra. He was curled on his side and sleeping peacefully. Declan found himself checking to make sure he was still breathing as a wave of unexpected terror washed over him. If anything happened to Ezra, Declan couldn't survive it. He couldn't force himself to leave Ezra alone. So he quietly climbed into bed with him. Icarus immediately stretched out between them and tried pushing him out of the bed. A soft laugh rumbled from Declan's throat. He wasn't the least bit surprised Icarus loved Ezra better. Unfortunately for Icarus, he was stuck with the both of them. Declan planned to dig his heels in now. If anyone was worth risking his entire life on, Ezra was the one. Declan was here for the long haul now. Ezra wouldn't know what hit him.

Thanks to the hospital pumping him full of fluids, Ezra found himself awake in the middle of the night. He had to pee, but Icarus and Declan were both sleeping peacefully beside him. He couldn't stop staring at the pair. Life was cruel, teasing him with the family he would never have. This life that wasn't his. This was how Ezra wanted to sleep every night. Well, maybe not with Icarus between them, but still.

Ezra's bladder screamed for him to move. With a sigh, Ezra rolled from the bed. Icarus immediately shot up and followed him. As Ezra stepped inside the bathroom, he froze. Thick brown paper covered the bathroom mirror, hiding his reflection. In black marker were huge words written where his mirror should be. "You don't need a mirror. You're beautiful."

With a shake of his head, Ezra headed for the toilet. He had forgotten about Declan doing the same thing when Ezra had battled this demon as a teenager. With his trip to the toilet out of the way, Ezra went through his usual bedtime routine. He brushed his teeth and moisturized before he changed into a pair of pajama pants. From there, he went on a hunt for Icarus's leash. He found all the puppy's things piled up by the back door next to Declan's suitcases. He snapped the leash in place and headed out. Icarus was too little to make it through the night yet. While he walked in circles with the dog, he tried not to think about anything too heavy. Maybe one day he would get a dog too. Back when his mom died and he had gone to live with Jessie, Ezra had fallen in love with Declan's huge Rottweiler, Lucifer. Unfortunately, after Lucifer died, Ezra hadn't wanted another full-time pet. Sitting with Lucifer while the vet put him to sleep had broken Ezra. It was too much loss too soon after losing his mom. He hadn't told Declan that, since he hadn't wanted Declan to have to be the one who sat with Lucifer while he died. Sometimes, life was just too heavy for Ezra. He didn't know how to be all things for everyone, but he wanted to make everyone happy. It was too bad that no one felt the same about him. Ezra was always alone, silently dying with no one to hold his hand.

Once Icarus had done all he was willing to do, Ezra turned back toward the house. He found Declan leaned in the doorway waiting.

"I'll install a doggie door so he can go out back when he wants."

Ezra wanted to point out Icarus and Declan didn't live there, but he had just considered getting a dog himself. In the end, it wasn't a big enough issue to argue about. "If that's what you want. The backyard is fenced in. My only issue would be the pool. I don't want him to fall in and drown."

"I'll get one of those pet ramps too, so he can get out if he finds himself in the water. We should probably add one of those pet watcher cameras too, as some extra protection."

Ezra shrugged. "Like I said, it's whatever you want to do."

Declan stooped and took off the puppy's leash, setting him free in the house. Icarus immediately hightailed it to his water bowl, making Ezra bite back a sigh. No doubt he would want to go out again soon. Ezra headed back to bed with Declan on his heels.

"I expected you to put up more of a fight at my suggestions."

Ezra climbed beneath the covers. His gaze never quite met Declan's. "No one ever cares what I want. I learned a long time ago to save my voice."

While Ezra watched with his tongue glued to roof of his mouth, Declan stripped down to his underwear and climbed into bed. "I care what you want."

"Then go home and leave me in peace."

Declan didn't as much as blink. "Are you at peace when I'm not around?"

"No."

To Ezra's surprise, Declan didn't show an ounce of triumph over Ezra's immediate answer. "Then I'm sorry, angel, but I can't go home."

Ezra didn't have the strength to argue. "Do you plan to sleep here from now on or are you waiting on me to assign you a room?"

Declan's gaze moved over Ezra's face as if reading his every reaction. "I'm a big boy. I could find a room for myself if I wanted, but I won't. This is my spot now."

Great. Ezra wasn't to be trusted to be alone, it seemed. "When you buy Icarus all his stuff for the backyard, get him a little staircase for the bed too. That way we don't have to lift him into bed every time he wants in."

Declan smiled. "That I can do."

Ezra would take it as a win, since Declan had already said he didn't want Icarus on the furniture. At least his desires weren't being completely discounted. He would take what he could get for now. "Did you sneak a peek at my latest magazine spread when I fell asleep?"

"Yes."

The unabashed way Declan copped to snooping had Ezra biting back a grin. "And?"

Declan took a ragged-sounding breath. "For real, you fuck with my head. I've never wanted anyone more."

Ezra tried not to be moved. "You can have it, if you want. The magazine, that is. I likely won't ever look at it."

A smile exploded across Declan's face. "You know I will."

Unexpectedly, Ezra's throat tightened. "You used to be my best friend." The confession came out in a harsh-sounding whisper.

Declan's smile disappeared. "Am I not anymore?"

Ezra shook his head. "You stopped trying a long time ago."

Declan blew out a shaky breath. "You definitely know how to always punch me in the heart."

"Am I wrong?"

Declan rolled onto his back and stared at the ceiling. "No. I don't know how to be just your friend anymore." He turned his head and met Ezra's stare again. "I'm sorry for that."

The lump in Ezra's throat made it almost

impossible for him to respond. He barely found his voice. "For what it's worth, I don't know how to be your friend anymore either. I don't know how to be okay with you touching anyone else."

"That's fair."

Ezra didn't know what that was supposed to mean, and he was too tired to dig. Instead, he closed his eyes against the sight of Declan's gorgeous face. The bed shifted. A smiled touched his lips as a furry body snuggled close. It meant a lot to him that Declan wasn't fighting him when it came to Icarus. Ezra was exhausted. He just wanted to rest and maybe steal some puppy snuggles. Everything else looked too hard at the moment.

THREE

Waiting for Ezra to wake up was hell. He knew Ezra needed sleep, but he also needed regular meals, and Declan was torn right down the middle. Jessie sent Johnny over to help Declan install a new doggy door and pool ramp, since Declan was set on doing it himself. Johnny also found the perfect bedside staircase for Icarus. Ezra slept through everything.

Right when Declan decided he would wake him, Ezra came padding into the living room, wearing a huge sweater, pajama pants, and looking like death. There were dark circles underneath his eyes, and he was pale. His hair stood in several directions and he somehow looked even skinnier today. Icarus didn't care about any of that. He ran circles around Ezra and scratched at his legs until Ezra picked him up. Declan fought a wince. He wasn't sure Ezra had the strength to carry the fat puppy around like a baby.

"Good morning, beautiful."

Ezra rolled his eyes as he headed for the couch and plopped down. "Is it morning?"

"It's one o'clock in the afternoon, actually."

An adorable hint of irritation crossed Ezra's features. "Why did you let me sleep so long?"

"You needed it." Declan stood. "Don't get comfortable." He moved Icarus from Ezra's lap and pulled him to his feet. "Your lunch is waiting."

"It's too late for lunch."

"We'll have a late dinner," Declan promised as he led Ezra to the kitchen and made him sit at the island. He opened the microwave and found the food he had stashed, waiting for Ezra to wake. "I ordered from your favorite burger place. It's probably cold, but you'll complain no matter what."

A hint of a smile crossed Ezra's features. "Just pop it back in the microwave for thirty seconds. It'll be okay."

Declan checked inside the bag to be certain there was nothing unsafe to nuke before doing as Ezra suggested. Once the thirty seconds were up, he passed the bag Ezra's way. To his surprise, Ezra ate without arguing. To give himself something to do other than watching Ezra's every move like a complete psychopath, Declan fixed Ezra something to drink.

He turned back toward the island to find Ezra feeding Icarus his fries. Declan bent and pretended to bang his head on the island. "Don't feed him that. Oh my god."

Not an ounce of guilt marred Ezra's face. "I just gave him a few. Look how happy they made him."

Declan glanced down at the dog. He looked extremely pleased with himself. Declan rubbed his temples. He didn't know how to fight these two. They outnumbered him. As if trying to make up for feeding the dog human food, Ezra made it through half the hamburger and part of the fries before his shoulders fell.

"I feel so disgusting. I need a shower, but I also don't think I have the energy. This is awful."

Since Declan hadn't expected Ezra to eat anything, he decided not to bitch about the half-eaten hamburger. "Come on. I'll stay in the bathroom with you and make sure you don't pass out."

As a testament to how bad Ezra felt, he didn't argue. "Okay." Declan's worry spiked even higher when he lifted Ezra into his arms and Ezra didn't fight him. He simply held Declan's neck and let everything happen to him.

Inside the bathroom, Declan set Ezra on his feet before heading for the shower. He fired the water to life. Declan played with the knobs until the ceiling rained down hot water.

"Make sure that's not too hot before you get in." He turned to find Ezra nude and waiting. Declan fought a hard battle, trying to keep his eyes locked on Ezra's face. He had seen nude photos of Ezra, but he had never seen him unclothed in person. His will was tested like never before as Ezra touched Declan's stomach, using Declan's body to steady himself, as he reached past him and felt of the water.

"It's fine." He stepped inside the shower, setting Declan free. Declan tried like hell to find something else to do, but he also needed to keep an eye on Ezra. In the end, he grabbed a chair from the vanity, set it beside the shower, and settled in to embrace his voyeurism.

In a small way, Ezra saved him. After a minute of attempting to get clean, he sat down on the seat built into the shower and cracked the shower door. As

Declan looked on, Ezra leaned back, turned his head, and held Declan's stare through the opening. With Ezra's hazel stare holding his, Declan wasn't as tempted to eye Ezra's body. Instead, he wanted to look into Ezra's soul.

"Why do I feel so bad?"

Declan's chest tightened at the question. "I don't know. Jessie is sending a doctor over today. Maybe he'll know."

Ezra nodded.

A desperate need to see Ezra smile overcame Declan. "Do you remember when Jessie flew us all to Ibiza for your eighteenth birthday?"

Ezra's shook his head and looked away. "You had so many men flirting with you. I spent the entire weekend outraged."

A chuckle slipped from Declan without his permission. "I couldn't see anyone but you. You brought all those brightly colored speedos with you and danced around me all weekend. I don't know why, but I think about that weekend a lot."

Ezra met his gaze again. "Do you want to know a secret about that weekend?"

Declan laughed, overwhelmed by sudden embarrassment. "Is it that your hotel balcony looked straight into my window and you watched me jack off? Because I know. I saw you. To my ever-living shame, that show was for you."

Not only did Ezra not crack a smile, he looked more serious than Declan had seen him in a long time. That was saying a lot, considering current circumstances. Ezra shook his head. "I planned to disappear that weekend."

Declan's smile fell. He blinked. "What?"

Ezra nodded. "I'd been planning it for a while. Two weeks earlier, I posed nude for a barely legal magazine and made a ton of money, because I have a famous brother. I opened a secret account with it and already had another shoot planned that would really set me up financially. I planned to take the money and slip away. Start a new life."

"Why?" Even Declan heard the horror in his single question.

A small smile touched Ezra's lips. He shrugged. "I didn't have any friends. Jessie was at the height of his drug use with no hope of stopping in sight. I wanted to be somewhere else. Be someone else. I already had a plane ticket to New York and my bags were packed when I watched you through your window, jacking off."

"Why didn't you leave?"

Ezra held Declan's stare. His heart was in his

eyes. "I was in love with you. You were the only piece of my life I couldn't leave behind." Ezra looked away. "If only I had known how much staying would hurt me."

"I don't know why you can't see things from my point of view." Declan didn't mean to lose his temper. It was all just so goddamn unfair. He couldn't take it any longer. "If I had followed my heart, I stood to lose everything. If I had touched my boss's little brother, I would have been blacklisted from ever doing this type of work again. I would've lost my chosen family. My friend. Then what if you'd decided you were only feeling your oats? Where would that have left me?"

Halfway through his speech, Ezra's gaze had latched on to him and hadn't moved. His expression stayed completely closed. "I've always seen your point of view," Ezra said, sounding calm. "That's why I never pushed. I kept waiting for you to finally realize that you're the one for me, and that I'm not the faint-of-heart type."

The truth struck Declan. He had known that. Ezra wasn't the type to play the field. He was serious and grounded. Ezra didn't sleep around, living wild and free. He knew himself and what he wanted. That meant Declan was the only one to blame.

Declan was the one who had been testing everyone else's waters.

"Could you help me out of here? My body feels like it weighs a ton. I don't know if I can stand."

Declan shot to his feet. He grabbed a towel, shut down the water, and started drying Ezra's body. Declan fought hard to keep it impersonal. His heart knew the truth, but Declan wouldn't make Ezra uncomfortable if he could help it. He gave Ezra the towel to hold on to and peeled off his shirt.

"We'll find you some real clothes in a bit, but this should keep you warm for now." He dressed Ezra like he was dressing a small child before scooping Ezra into his arms. The shirt looked like a dress on Ezra, but Ezra didn't complain. Ezra tried drying his hair with the towel while Declan set him in the chair he had vacated.

"It'll be impossible for me to fix my hair with the mirrors covered."

Declan shrugged. "You look fine now, but I could do it for you. God knows, I've studied your every feature enough to know how you usually look."

A small smile touched Ezra's lips. "Have at it."

With a sharp nod, Declan grabbed a brush and worked on getting rid of any tangles. He traded it for a comb when it came time to style. "Which products do you use?"

"Just that," Ezra answered, pointing at a pink jar.

Feeling less than confident, Declan opened the jar. It smelled like Ezra. He scooped some out and tried forcing Ezra's hair to stay in the shape it usually held. It wasn't working. Ezra made his style look so effortless. Declan was failing. Eventually, he gave up. It wasn't like Ezra could see himself anyhow, and Declan thought Ezra was beautiful no matter what.

"Um, there. I guess it's good enough."

Ezra eyed him like he saw through Declan's words to the truth. "How bad is it?"

Giving in, Declan found a handheld mirror and let Ezra look at himself. He held his breath as Ezra turned his head from side to side, inspecting the mess Declan had made. After a moment, a snort escaped Ezra. He set the mirror aside and covered his face. Just when Declan started to panic, he realized Ezra was laughing. His entire body shook with it. His laughter grew bigger by the second until he was howling. A smile stretched Declan's lips. He truly had made a crazy hot mess out of Ezra's hair. Unexpectedly, Declan's throat swelled. He hadn't seen Ezra laugh in forever. In fact, he couldn't recall the last time he had seen Ezra smile and mean it.

Declan dropped to his knees at Ezra's feet. He wrapped his arms around Ezra, buried his face against his stomach, and held on. Declan had been killing the thing he loved for so long that he didn't know if he could save them, but he had to. He needed Ezra's smiles and laughter.

Ezra rubbed every place he could reach, as if trying to soothe Declan. "It's okay, sweetie. It's just hair. Would you like to try putting makeup on me next? That could be fun."

The backs of Declan's eyes burned. He had been so in love with Ezra for so long, he couldn't fight this. Watching Ezra collapse last night had been the final straw. He didn't want to lose Jessie's friendship and he loved his job. But nothing mattered as much as Ezra to Declan.

Ezra squeezed his shoulders and felt up his biceps. "Jesus, Declan. How many hours a day do you work out?"

A choked laugh escaped Declan. "Not as many as you'd think. I'm naturally big. It's genetics."

Ezra traced a cut line of Declan's arm. "This is not genetics. It's hard work, and I just meant that I've never seen you work out. How is that possible? We've spent a lot of time together over the years."

Declan couldn't relax his hold. He settled on his

ass and laid his head in Ezra's lap. "I've never seen you do your hair, obviously, but I know you do it."

"We should change that sometime." Ezra ran his fingers through Declan's hair and massaged his scalp. "You should watch me do my hair and I should watch you lift weights. I think I've been missing bits and pieces of your life that I don't want to miss."

The burning behind Declan's eyes increased. For the first time, he truly understood that Ezra loved him as much as he loved Ezra. Staying silent and protecting his own ass hadn't been hurting only him. Ezra had been trying to make him see that. He didn't understand why this one moment finally broke through, but it did.

"Do you still think about running away?"

Ezra didn't stop playing with his hair. "All the time, but everywhere I go, I'm still me. I can't run from what I hate the most."

Declan didn't know how to fight that. "I'll take you back to bed. You're probably ready to fall out." Declan pushed to his knees.

"Will you stay with me?"

It wasn't like Declan could deny Ezra anything. He scooped Ezra from the chair. "Of course."

"Can I keep your shirt for now?"

A chuckle escaped Declan. "It's yours." As he

set Ezra on the bed, Ezra scooted over to make room for him. Declan didn't hesitate to climb in beside him and tug Ezra into his arms. He forced himself not to think about Ezra wearing nothing but his shirt and how easy it would be to sneak beneath it. The doorbell chimed, saving Declan from himself.

Ezra groaned. "I thought I would finally get some cuddles."

A smile tugged at Declan's lips. He kissed Ezra's shoulder. "Later. That's probably the doctor." He rushed from the bed to answer the door.

A blond guy who looked way too young to be a doctor stood on the other side. He smiled brightly at Declan. "Hey. I'm Dr. Black. Jessie sent me to see Ezra."

Ezra was only wearing a shirt. This wasn't the old dude Ezra had seen last time he got sick. Declan wanted to slam the door in his face. He didn't. Declan stepped aside and motioned the doctor inside. "Hey. Yeah. Ezra's in bed. He managed enough energy to get up and eat earlier, but it was zapped pretty quickly." He closed the door and headed down the hall with the doctor trailing in his wake. "His bedroom is this way." Declan didn't speak again until they were inside Ezra's bedroom.

Ezra was sitting up, leaned back against his pillows and headboard, waiting.

He smiled at the sight of the doctor. "Hey, Seth."

Oh, great. They were on a first-name basis.

Seth smiled like his entire life was made better by seeing Ezra. "Hey, Ezra. I hear you've been causing trouble."

Declan motioned absently behind him toward the door. "I'll just close this and leave you two alone."

Ezra flashed him a grateful smile. Declan ducked out. He forced himself not to listen at the door and instead headed to the kitchen. As he caught sight of Icarus's food bowl, he realized he hadn't seen the dog since Ezra fed him fries. Declan searched every place he could think to check before looking out back. He found Icarus stretched out on his back, fat belly soaking up the sun, and with what was left of Ezra's hamburger still plastered to his chunky little face. Declan dug out his phone and snapped a picture before heading back inside. He had to figure out how the little asshole had gotten on the counter. It seemed Icarus was thrilled with his new home.

In the kitchen, he found a mess around the island. He had no idea how Icarus had managed to climb up there, but he had enjoyed a feast. Declan cleaned up while trying not to think about Ezra being half nude and alone with Dr. Smexy M.D.

"You're Declan, right?"

Declan tried hiding the way Seth startled him. The dude walked too softly. "Yep. That's me."

Seth nodded. His blue eyes did have the perfect amount of genuine concern for a doctor. Declan would give him that. "Ezra gave me permission to discuss his health with you since it seems you've volunteered to be his support system through this."

That made Declan feel a thousand percent better. "Okay. Why is he still so wiped? In the shower, he said he didn't have the energy to stand."

Seth set an old-timey-looking doctors' bag on the island. It caught Declan's eye. He hadn't even noticed the guy carrying it inside. Declan had to force his attention back to Seth's face. It wasn't like Declan to be so unobservant. "Going by his lab results from the ER last night, I'd say he's still suffering from vitamin deficiency. I gave him a couple of shots that should help. Plus, I've called him in a few prescriptions. You should probably call the pharmacy and arrange to have those delivered."

Declan nodded along, waiting his turn so he could ask what he wanted to know the most. "How bad are things this time?"

"Not as bad as they look," Seth said, surprising Declan. "He's pretty self-aware. This wasn't purposeful. He admits he stopped taking his antidepressants about a year ago and thought he would be fine. Meds can trick you into thinking you're well. He lost his appetite a couple of months ago when the depression struck hard, but he's been trying to keep eating. I don't think this is a relapse of the anorexia as much as it is the depression. Still, one thing feeds the other. So he needs to get back on his meds. I think he'll be okay. After all, he's already agreed to accept help and that's a hurdle most people won't jump."

"Is he safe to travel?"

Seth's eyebrows rose. It was obvious Declan had surprised him since Ezra wouldn't have said anything about traveling... since he didn't know. "He should be good as long he follows my instructions." He nodded as if the idea solidified in his mind. "Honestly, it might be good for him. There's no reason he can't do his counseling via televisits. Getting out of the house and this slump might be exactly what he needs to kickstart recovery."

That was exactly what Declan needed to hear. "Thank you. I'll make sure he stays on task."

A flirtatious smile touched the doctor's lips,

taking Declan by surprise. "You look like you can handle the job."

Declan didn't smile back. "I can. Nothing matters to me except Ezra's well-being. I'll walk you to the door."

Seth grabbed his bag and headed that way without waiting for Declan. "I know my way. You should get back to Ezra. Don't hesitate to call if you need anything."

At the mention of getting back to Ezra, Declan stopped listening. His feet were already headed that way. He hadn't been lying. Nothing mattered to him except Ezra. Maybe Declan had spent a lot of years fighting against his heart, but he wouldn't be making that mistake any longer. It was time for Ezra to get well. He would need his strength if he wanted to fend off any of the love Declan intended to throw his way. It was time to settle this.

Declan almost made it back to the bedroom before the doorbell rang again. With a growl, he changed directions. He tried tempering his reaction as he yanked open the door, in case the doctor had forgotten something. Wrecker stood on the other side.

Wrecker's eyes flashed with something

dangerous. "What have you done with Ezra? He's not answering his phone."

Declan was a big guy. He didn't doubt his ability to take down any challenger, but Wrecker wasn't small either. The dude would put up a good fight. "He's sleeping."

"Go get him. I want to see with my own eyes that he's okay."

"You'll have to take my word for it," Declan said, refusing to back down.

A hint of humor tinged Wrecker's features, but Declan wasn't fooled. It was an act meant to knock Declan off balance. "Here's the thing, *friend*, maybe everyone else thinks you're the harmless bodyguard just looking out for his boss's little brother, but I know different. See, I notice things when I leave work and pass this house. I see how the same black truck parked in his driveway now is always parked just down the street. My keen eyes don't miss you sitting behind the wheel, watching Ezra. Following him. I've got your number. So you need to produce Ezra now, or maybe I'll make a trip to Jessie's instead. I think he'd be interested to know his bodyguard is dangerous in a way he never expected."

Declan thought to play it off and pretend Wrecker was wrong, but he wasn't, and Declan was doomed to lose that game. He changed tactics. "I can't let you disturb Ezra. He was just released from the hospital."

Something flickered in Wrecker's eyes and Declan saw the truth. Wrecker truly did see all and know all. He wasn't surprised Ezra was sick. "What happened?"

"People like you happened," Declan said, going for the jugular. "You're with him damn near every day and *see things.*" Declan barely stopped himself from making air quotes, but he knew his tone had done it for him. "Before I showed up last night, he hadn't eaten in god knows how long before he fell out, dehydrated and completely depleted of vitamins. I thought you were watching him. You claim to have his back. Why didn't you go to Jessie with that? Or am I the only problem you see with Ezra's life?"

"Jessie has been out of town." Wrecker said the words quietly—like it broke him that he hadn't been able to get Ezra help. Like he hadn't known where else to turn. His gaze turned inward for a moment before he focused on Declan again. "Tell him I stopped by. If I don't hear from him by the end of the night, I'm going to Jessie."

Declan shrugged. "Fair enough." He shut the

door in Wrecker's face. Declan planned to be gone with Ezra before the end of the night anyhow. Maybe they would stay gone for good. Declan was tired of worrying about what everyone else would think. So he wouldn't anymore.

FOUR

EZRA WOKE ON A SHARP GASP, LEAVING BEHIND A nightmare he forgot the instant his eyes opened. He had fallen asleep almost the minute the doctor left. Ezra had been having a hard time keeping his eyes open through his shower. The second he had finally been alone, the life had seeped from him. Now he stared at his surroundings, incapable of understanding his change in locations.

"What the... fluff? Where are we?"

Declan glanced his way from his spot behind the wheel. "You don't remember? You woke up enough to get dressed."

Ezra blinked. He didn't remember that at all. Dang. He had truly passed out. They were in Declan's truck and headed down the interstate. Ezra was dressed... sort of. He still wore Declan's huge shirt and a pair of short shorts. It was dark. Ezra glanced at the clock. It was two. He assumed, judging by the pitch-black sky, it was two in the morning.

"Where are we going?" he asked again when his mind turned up blank.

"Mesa, Arizona."

For a moment, Ezra tried harder to remember agreeing to go to Arizona. Still, the last memory he had was his doctor's visit. "Why are we going to Arizona?"

A sexy rumble of laughter fell from Declan's lips. "Because it's beautiful there and you need a vacation. I got us a private place right near some great hiking trails. Your prescriptions are filled. Our bags are packed. We're ditching reality for a while."

"You packed me a bag."

Even though it hadn't been a question, Declan obviously took it as one. "No. Jessie and Theo stopped by to check on you, but you were too out of it to visit. When I talked to them about this trip, Jessie agreed it was a good idea and Theo volunteered to pack for you."

"Oh. That's fine, then. He knows what I need."

Declan snorted. "Did you think I would screw it up?"

Ezra rushed to make things better. He hadn't meant his words as an insult. "No. It's not that. Theo's lived with me recently. He knows my daily habits and whatnot. I just meant that he would know what to pack."

Another sexy chuckle escaped Declan. "I'm not insulted, angel."

Before Ezra could argue that he had sounded insulted, Declan exited the interstate. "We need to stop to walk Icarus."

Ezra glanced behind him. Icarus was asleep on the floorboard behind the driver's seat. Ezra heard himself admitting something he never planned to say. "I was scared to death when I gave Icarus to you at Christmas. I thought I might be overstepping and hurting you." Declan had lost a dog that was his baby and hadn't tried getting another dog since. Ezra had taken a huge risk giving Declan Icarus. He hadn't known how Declan would react.

Declan didn't look his way. He kept his eyes on the road and his voice sounded hesitant. "After Lucifer died, I didn't want another pet of any kind. If anyone else had given me one, there's a chance I would've turned him down." Declan quickly glanced his way. "But it's you. If you'd handed me a snake, I would've loved it, because I love you. Icarus is perfect, though. He makes us like a little family."

Ezra turned inside himself. He didn't know what to think. For years, they had gone back and forth. They would get close and Ezra would think they were finally going to be together, only to have Declan shove him away again. Ezra didn't have the strength to handle that right now. But Declan kept saying he loved Ezra and he had kissed Ezra, which was more than Ezra ever expected. The hope building in his chest scared the hell out of him. The issue churned in his mind all the way to Mesa until he exhausted himself again. When Declan pulled into the driveway of a tiny cottage, Ezra sat forward and eyed the place. It was really, really small but adorable. It was like a gem in the wild. There was nothing surrounding them except beautiful scenery. Even though the house was minuscule, there was a pool out back. The entire place was surrounded by a fence. It looked like a getaway spot.

Inside the house, Ezra realized something else. They would be sharing a much smaller bed. The place was nothing more than a queen-sized bed, a small eating area, a kitchen, and a bathroom. There was no TV or anything meant for entertainment.

There was a jacuzzi tub in the bathroom but no shower. The mirrors were already covered, making Ezra wonder how Declan had pulled this off. It seemed they would be roughing it, to Ezra's standards. Ezra didn't argue. A part of him recognized this was exactly what he needed. A place to be still and quiet. This place made the world look smaller and easier to manage. Declan knew him too well.

Declan dragged a huge cooler inside. "I tried packing up most of the groceries Johnny brought by. There's no sense in letting anything go to waste. I'll bring your suitcase in next so you can do whatever you need."

"I can help. Put me to work."

Declan shook his head. "I've got this. You're supposed to be resting."

"What about you?" Ezra couldn't stop the question. "I don't think you've really slept since I landed in the ER. Maybe you should be the one relaxing."

Declan stared at him in a way Ezra couldn't decipher. He seemed closed off, yet he couldn't completely hide the heat in his eyes. "I'm good. Just let me get everything inside and we'll go to bed."

Icarus scratched at Ezra's legs, demanding his

attention. Ezra absently picked him up and rubbed his head while trying to work out Declan's mood. He didn't shake himself from his stupor until Declan brought in their luggage. The tiny house got smaller with them and all their stuff inside. To give himself something to do, Ezra set up Icarus's dog bowls and toys before going to work on emptying the cooler. To Ezra's surprise, Declan didn't argue with him helping. Instead, he disappeared inside the bathroom with a small bag. Declan re-emerged a few minutes later, wearing nothing but workout shorts. Ezra fought himself. His gaze kept sliding toward Declan's beautiful body. He was just too big. Ezra couldn't avoid looking at him. He fought for anything to say or do to keep from looking like the obsessed fool he had always been for Declan.

"Your feet will probably hang off that tiny bed."

Declan shrugged. "I'm used to being too big for my surroundings. It'll be okay." He flashed Ezra a devilish smile as he turned down the covers. "Plus, you won't be able to escape me. There are all sorts of benefits to cuddling, according to research. Cuddling makes people happier, strengthens our immune systems, relieves anxiety, and promotes good sleep patterns."

Ezra's cheeks ached from smiling. "I have a hard time picturing you reading articles about cuddling."

"What do you imagine me doing in my spare time?"

Ezra grabbed his toiletries bag and eased his way toward the bathroom. "I don't know." Ezra practically leapt into the bathroom and shut himself away before he said something stupid. What he imagined Declan doing in his spare time always depended upon Ezra's mood. If he was angry with Declan, he assumed Declan spent all his time chasing other men. If he was in one of his longing moods, he pictured Declan pining for him too. A lot of ridiculous thoughts went through Ezra's head all day long. All of them were better left unsaid. After all, there was nowhere for Ezra to hide in this small getaway house. The less Ezra embarrassed himself on this trip, the better. He was too old to runaway now. But he still might if he humiliated himself too much right now. Ezra didn't have the strength to stay and fight.

DECLAN KILLED THE LIGHTS AND CLIMBED INTO bed. Icarus immediately started whining. He stopped the second Declan helped him into bed. It seemed Declan had already lost the battle when it came to Icarus always sleeping with them. It wouldn't be easy in this small bed. This wasn't the first time he had stayed in this getaway house. In fact, he knew the owner. That was the only way he had managed to get the place on such short notice, and he got the mirrors covered before Ezra arrived. He hoped this quiet time away, sequestered with Ezra, Declan could help Ezra get better while also winning him for good. This was a make them or break them trip. There were no distractions here. No place for Ezra to hide. By the end of this trip, Declan would know the right thing to do. He would know whether Ezra was better off with or without him. Either way, he would be unemployed. Declan couldn't go back to working for Jessie now. Ezra was the love of his life. He either had to be with him or remove himself completely from Ezra's life. It was well past the time he should have accepted he was part of Ezra's problems and fix it. Not to mention, Ezra wasn't the only one suffering. Declan couldn't take the pain anymore either. He wanted more.

The bathroom door opened. "Holy shot. It's really dark in here."

Declan smiled at the sound of Ezra's voice.

Damn. He really loved everything about him. Declan rolled and snagged his cellphone, lighting a path to the bed. "This way." Once Ezra made it to the edge of the bed, Declan set the phone aside, snagged Ezra's waist, and rolled. He tucked Ezra into bed and against his body in one swift motion before tugging the covers over them. Icarus settled down across their entangled feet.

Ezra relaxed into his hold.

Declan's body responded immediately, going painfully hard. There was no way Ezra missed the erection pressed against his ass, but he didn't call Declan on it.

"It's so quiet in here," Ezra whispered.

It really was. Ezra had a sound machine in his room. While Declan had noticed that before, he hadn't thought anything of it until now. It was a new detail of Ezra that Declan wanted. He rolled and grabbed his cellphone again. It only took him a second to find a sound machine app, download it, and the sound of the ocean filled the room. He settled back down, holding Ezra. "There. Now you shouldn't have any trouble sleeping."

He felt Ezra's body shake—like silent laughter rolled through him. "Except for that erection that keeps tapping me like it's trying to get my attention."

"You can ignore that."

Ezra rolled in his arms and draped his leg over Declan's body so he could scoot as close as possible. "There. That's better."

Fuck. It really was not. Ezra still wore Declan's t-shirt and he was back to having nothing on underneath. He was hard too and their bodies were pressed together. This was hell. It was heaven. Declan was torn in two.

Ezra tilted up his chin and touched his lips to Declan's. Declan caved. He rolled, bringing Ezra with him, leaving Ezra straddling his body. Declan held the back of Ezra's head as he kissed Ezra deep, trying hard to get closer. He wanted to taste Ezra's tongue and come away with Ezra's love. There was no one else out there for him. Ezra moved restlessly against him, shoving at Declan's shorts. He swore he felt Ezra's triumph when his erection sprang free. Declan's entire body nearly jackknifed from the bed when their cocks collided. Ezra's hips rolled. He rocked against Declan's body. Declan's fingers dug into Ezra's hips as he tried controlling the pace. He didn't want this to ever end. Unfortunately, his body knew it was Ezra—the man he had loved and ached for—moving against him. Declan tore his mouth away and squeezed his eyes closed, trying to fight the growing pressure climbing his cock.

Ezra kissed his neck. "This is what I do in my spare time. I picture you beneath me just like this."

A loud pant burst from Declan at Ezra's confession. It was like his spirit left his body as ecstasy rocked him. A spasm made his entire body jerk. Hot cum slicked his skin. He had never blown so fast in his life. It was almost embarrassing, but he was too in love to feel anything else. His emotions choked him. He kissed Ezra so hard and deep that he couldn't have said if Ezra came or not. His mind was too big of a mess. It wasn't the romantic encounter he always dreamed they would have, considering how sweet Ezra was. Instead, it had more or less just happened. In fact, the encounter had been so natural that Declan felt incredibly stupid for constantly fighting himself.

Their kiss turned sweet until Declan was smiling so hard against Ezra's lips that he could hardly keep up. "I feel dumb, but you short-circuited my brain and I don't even know if you came."

Ezra chuckled. "Surely you don't think you made this big of a mess alone."

Declan swiped his lips across Ezra's again. "I

don't know," he admitted, still barely comprehending a thing. "I can't feel anything below my heart."

For a moment, Ezra kissed him so sweetly that the backs of Declan's eyes stung. Then Ezra went in for the kill, decimating what was left of Declan's defenses. "I love you, sexy protector. It's always only been you for me."

It was like a sucker punch to the chest. Ezra had always sneaked beneath his shell by making Declan feel like he was the strongest man in the world—like no one could keep Jessie and him safe better than Declan. For someone who had grown up feeling helpless, it was empowering as hell. It was addictive. Ezra made him want to be the best and most protective man to prove him right. He would prove him right. By the time they left here, Ezra would know he was loved and cherished if it was the last fucking thing Declan did. He owed Ezra that much.

FIVE

A very nude Ezra filled the spot next to Declan in the bed. With the sun lighting the room, Declan couldn't stop staring at him. After taking Icarus for a walk and filling his bowls, Declan had returned to bed to find Ezra had kicked away the blankets. With his head buried beneath his pillow, his entire back and ass were on full display. Declan's feet were glued to the floor as he stared down at him. When he had sat with Ezra while Ezra showered, Declan had tried his ass off not to think about Ezra's nudity. That moment had been about taking care of him. This moment was different. Declan couldn't tear his eyes away from what Ezra had done to himself. Every bone in his back was visible. He looked like someone on the edge of death. Each breath Declan took came harder and harder as the truth sank in. If he hadn't shown up when he had, Ezra would have died. Not could have. He would have. Declan wouldn't have been there to help when Ezra collapsed. Ezra would have simply slipped away while no one was the wiser. The scariest part of that was the truth. Declan knew that had been the point. Ezra hadn't wanted to go on living.

Declan shook his head at the thought. He couldn't go there. Ezra meant too much to Declan's sanity. He forced his feet to move away from the bed. Ezra needed sleep. He needed food and rest. Declan would make sure he got them. He headed for the bathroom and went to work filling the tub. As much as he wished this place had a shower, he was grateful the jacuzzi tub was large enough for someone his size. No showers or tubs usually fit him. He was too tall and wide for this world. Declan ducked through doorways and sat uncomfortably in chairs. Bathtubs were usually a no go for him. Luckily, this one fit him and then some. So he would enjoy it and let Ezra rest, but he would leave the bathroom door open too just in case.

As he waited for the tub to fill, he checked his

phone. He had missed four calls from Jessie and a text message. He opened the message.

Jessie: *Why did Wrecker come by this morning claiming you've been stalking Ezra, and now you're refusing to let him see Ezra?*

Declan swiped his hands over his face, suppressing a growl. He had truly hoped Wrecker was bluffing about going to Jessie. He paced for a minute, trying to decide what to do. Finally, he just started typing with no plan at all.

Declan: *I don't know, man. Wrecker stopped by before we left town. He demanded I let him in to see Ezra. Ezra was still sleeping, and I didn't want to bother him. So I told him to hold off until Ezra contacted him. I guess that wasn't good enough.*

While staring at his phone, Declan held his breath. He didn't breathe properly again until Jessie got back to him.

Jessie: *All right. I've always liked Wrecker, but he said some crazy shit. He claimed he had seen you sitting outside Ezra's house several times and you had been showing up at The Back Porch every night, harassing Ezra. It all sounded nuts to me, but I had to ask. Wrecker's been good to Ezra and Theo. It seemed an odd accusation to come from nowhere.*

Declan: *I've been to The Back Porch several*

times. Just like everyone else. But I would think Ezra would tell you if he felt harassed. As for my truck sitting outside Ezra's house, I guess it's possible he's seen me picking him up or dropping him off. Or, hell, it's a black truck. It looks like a million others. It's entirely possible he thinks he's in the right, but I've done nothing that I can think of to give him the idea that Ezra is any danger with me. Maybe he's jealous?

Jessie: *True. He did have that jilted lover tone about him. I guess just keep me posted on Ezra's health and tell him to call me. I've been texting him, but he's not responding.*

Declan: *Will do. He's been sleeping almost nonstop. I'll give him another hour and then I'll get him up and have him call you.*

Jessie: *Nah. Don't wake him. Just let him know when he gets up on his own. I know you'll take good care of him. You always have.*

Declan: *Yep. I've got him. Talk to you later.*

Declan tossed the phone aside. Fucking Wrecker, sticking his nose in other people's business. Ezra would talk to the guy when he talked to him, but it was Declan's time with Ezra right now. He knew he was crazy when it came to Ezra. Declan didn't need anyone else pointing that out. He let it go and climbed into the tub and started scrubbing. With the jets going, his shampoo and body wash turned the top half of the water into bubbles. His muscles relaxed. Declan closed his eyes and leaned his head back, letting the tension in his muscles drain away. The water shifted. Ezra climbed into the opposite end of the tub and sat between Declan's feet. He pulled his knees up to his chest and openly stared at Declan while Declan stared back through half-closed lids.

"Did you sleep okay?" Even Declan heard the gravelly edge to his voice—like lust filled him already from Ezra's presence alone.

Ezra nodded. "Did you? I've been in here for a minute. I even brushed my teeth, and you didn't stir. For a second, I thought you had passed out."

Damn. It was possible he had dozed off and hadn't realized it. Between Ezra's health scare and Wrecker's threats, Declan had been on edge for days. "I spent the whole night savoring the fact that you were in my arms. You have no idea how long I've wanted that."

Ezra hid a smile against his knees.

Declan sat up. "Come here." Declan urged Ezra closer and went to work scrubbing his body. He bathed Ezra like he would a child, washing his hair and body. Ezra tolerated him without complaint.

Declan relished every second. Once he had Ezra clean, he tugged Ezra forward until Ezra straddled his lap. Then he leaned back again with Ezra cuddled against his chest. Ezra settled down into his arms. Their bodies molded together.

"It's still funny to me that you're such a big guy and you chose this tiny house."

"There's nowhere for you to go here," Declan admitted as he skimmed his lips across Ezra's temple. "You can't escape me here."

Ezra didn't respond. He simply lingered in Declan's arms like he knew it was where he belonged. "You're hard for me again," Ezra said after a few minutes, sounding sleepy.

"I'm always hard for you. You'll have to learn to ignore that."

Ezra chuckled. The small sound vibrated against Declan's chest.

Declan needed to change the subject. "Are you feeling up to going out? There's an awesome all-you-can-eat breakfast place not too far from here. It's close to a shopping center I think you would like." Declan knew he would have to sweeten food with some other prize, since Ezra still wasn't showing any signs of having an appetite.

"That's fine."

Declan wasn't dumb. He knew he needed to act quickly on Ezra's agreement. His mood might change any second. Declan held Ezra to his chest and stood. With a laugh, Ezra wrapped his legs around Declan and held on while Declan climbed from the tub. Once he was out of the tub with no chance of falling, Declan found his feet glued to the floor. He couldn't take another step. The sound of Ezra's laughter was too much for his heart.

"In case I haven't said so, and you're still not understanding what's happening here, I'm completely in love with you."

Ezra's features softened. "I love you too."

"Then kiss me." Declan couldn't stop the demand if he tried.

Ezra didn't hesitate to press his lips to Declan's. Declan swore his body temperature immediately rose by ten degrees. No one had ever made him burn the way Ezra did. It was like they were more than meant to be. They belonged together on some higher plane—like soul mates. When Ezra's tongue stroked his, Declan's knees weakened. Before falling for Ezra, Declan hadn't known someone could feel so strongly about another person.

"I've decided I don't want to ignore your erection."

Declan headed for the bed at Ezra's claim, uncaring if they were both still soaking wet. His knees wouldn't hold out with too much talk like that from Ezra. Icarus chased his feet. Declan couldn't think about him right now. Ezra needed his attention. A thought hit him as he set Ezra on the bed. "You're not trying to get out of eating, are you?"

Ezra shook his head. "We'll still go out. I promise. Right now, though, I really need you to make love to me."

Every muscle in Declan's body jerked. He swore a shot of electricity went through him at Ezra's claim. He held up a finger. "Hold that thought." Declan scooped up the dog and locked him in the bathroom before heading for his bag. He had condoms and lube packed, because he always had those things ready to go. He grabbed both and headed back toward the bed. Icarus whined and scratched at the door. Declan pinched the spot between his eyes. With a chuckle, Ezra sat up, grabbed his phone, and after a few clicks, music filled the air, drowning out the puppy.

"Works for me," Declan said, climbing onto the bed. He stalked Ezra until he could snag his waist and twist. On his back, he settled Ezra on his hips. "Kiss me again." Declan could hear the neediness in his voice. He didn't care. For years, he had dreamed of making love to Ezra. Not once did those dreams include loud music and a whining dog, but Declan gave no fucks about perfection at the moment. All Declan cared about was Ezra. He was the only necessity now.

Ezra lowered his head and captured Declan's lips. He kissed Declan deeply. Declan could feel Ezra's love. It was overwhelming and humbling. Possessiveness and protectiveness filled Declan's chest. He wanted to be gentle, taking care of Ezra's fragile health. At the same time, he wanted to fuck Ezra hard enough he seared his name on Ezra's soul. Instead, he let Ezra take the lead.

He felt Ezra smile against his lips. "If you want me to have any energy left for the day, you'll need to do some of the work here."

A laugh rose and caught in Declan's throat. It seemed he would need to find that middle ground after all. Declan rolled to his side. "I don't want to hurt you."

Ezra looked so trusting. "You won't."

Declan fumbled with the condom and lube. Once he was suited up and slick, he urged Ezra onto his side, facing away from him before dragging his ass closer. Ezra clutched at the sheets as Declan toyed with his asshole. He stretched and lubed, making sure Ezra was ready before easing inside. Ezra moaned like he had never had anything better. Declan found himself drawing Ezra back against his chest. There was no skill or practiced pace. Declan simply moved, rocking inside Ezra as he held him close. Ezra reached up and held the back of Declan's head as Declan sucked and kissed Ezra's neck. In his heart, Declan knew this one moment wouldn't last forever, but he wanted to remember it forever. Ezra was hot and tight. Every sound he made drove Declan insane. All those things were secondary to how Declan felt. He was overcome.

His eyes burned and his throat hurt. This was Ezra. He finally, finally had the one thing in the world he wanted most—the love of his life in his arms. It felt like victory—like his dreams coming true. He needed Ezra to feel the same. Declan's fingers encircled Ezra's cock. He massaged, pumping and tugging. Ezra squirmed against him, as if he didn't know whether to ride Declan's hand or dick. Declan didn't take mercy on him. He needed Ezra to be as big of a mess as him.

Ezra moaned.

Declan nearly came. He tried coaxing Ezra into

orgasm. "That's it, gorgeous. Come for me. I want to hear it. I want to see it."

Ezra's body stiffened, dragging a cry from Declan as his asshole squeezed him tight. A spasm rocked Ezra before his body tried sucking Declan deeper. His cock twitched in Declan's hand. An orgasm hit Declan so hard, he lost the ability to hear. His lungs seized as he pumped the condom full of cum. Declan held Ezra tight, trying not to hurt him as he savored every second of ecstasy. He wasn't giving this up. Not now. Not ever. They were beautiful together. Declan would do whatever it took to make Ezra better so they could have as many years together as possible. This was the forever kind of love. Ezra would see it too. Declan would make sure of it.

They didn't make it out in time for breakfast, but they found a nice Mexican restaurant and Ezra was miserably full of cheese dip. He was tired again, but he kept putting one foot in front of the other. The shopping center was nice, and Declan kept taking his hand. Ezra wasn't ready to go back to the house yet. He hadn't felt this free in a long time.

"You need these in your life."

Ezra turned his head to find Declan holding out a pair of diva-sized sunglasses with glittery sequins on the sides.

With a chuckle, Ezra accepted and popped them on his face. "How do I look?"

Going by Declan's huge smile, he looked ridiculous. "Beautiful."

"Oh my god. Is that Ra Lee? It is."

Ezra froze at the name. He pulled off the sunglasses and turned his head. Ezra cringed when he spotted the two women headed his way. He considered jumping behind Declan and forcing Declan to play the bodyguard. Instead, he squared his shoulders, pasted on his best smile, and waited for the inevitable.

"I can't believe it's you. I was just showing Meg one of your videos."

"Hi," Ezra said for lack of anything more intelligent.

Declan took turns looking between him and the two women who had run him down. Ezra didn't alleviate Declan's curiosity.

The blond of the two pulled out her cellphone. "Can I get a picture with you? My son will just die. That's who introduced me to your channel."

"Sure."

Ezra smiled while taking pictures with both women. He knew without looking that he looked like hell, and—no doubt—these pictures would be all over the internet in less than an hour.

The brunette motioned Declan's way with pure interest flashing in her eyes. "Is this your boyfriend or your bodyguard?"

Declan didn't wait for an introduction. He stepped forward and wrapped his arm around Ezra's waist. "Both, actually. I'm Declan."

Both women looked from Declan to Ezra. "Wow," they said simultaneously, making Ezra laugh.

Ezra fought to hide his shock over Declan's declaration. "I know. He's overwhelming."

"That's one way of putting it," the blonde said while the brunette nodded.

Ezra stood still and listened to the women speak. He ended up autographing a few things before they finally moved on. Ezra held his breath. He knew what would come next and he wasn't wrong.

"Ra Lee, huh? What the hell? How did I not know you have a whole other identity?"

With a shrug, Ezra tried to play it off like it was no big deal. "I have to do something with my time. It's not like I lounge by the pool all day and transform into a socialite by night. You know that's not me. I had to find something productive to do. So, my friend Brett. You know him. The YouTube producer. He said I should try to capitalize more on my sense of fashion. I let him record a few videos of me repurposing outfits for different occasions, and—to my surprise—they took off. Obviously, I didn't want to use my real name. So I went with a combination of what Brett has always called me, Ra, and my middle name, Lee. I never thought anyone would watch anything I did. It seems I was wrong." Ezra felt a wicked smile shape his lips. "I'm glad to know I can still surprise you, though. Of course, I'm just as shocked to learn you're my boyfriend now."

Declan flashed him a sexy smile. "Well, I mean, you've been in my pants. You should give me some title."

"Everyone has been in your pants. I'm not special." The words were out there before Ezra could stop them. Declan's smile slipped away, making it harder for Ezra to breathe.

Declan looked away. "What would you like to do next? There are a few mini-golf places around here."

"I'm sorry. I shouldn't have said that."

Declan still didn't look his way. "Of course you should have. I've spent the last six years, since you turned eighteen and moved out, sleeping with everyone. You've spent the last six years showing your nude body to everyone. There's no sense in pretending. Right?"

Ouch. Ezra didn't know what to say, so he didn't say anything. He had posed nude for a few different magazines. But the comparison wasn't the same. No one had ever understood him. Ezra had always thought—maybe—Declan did. It seemed he had been wrong.

"Now I'm the one who's sorry," Declan said, sounding apologetic.

Ezra didn't respond. He wasn't trying to make Declan feel guilty. Ezra just truly didn't know how to express something he had honestly thought Declan already understood. Declan took a breath, as if he meant to say more. Ezra cut him off. "I don't like myself."

Declan snapped his mouth closed so hard that Ezra heard it happen.

Once the truth was out there, Ezra didn't stop. It was easier because they were walking side by side and Declan wasn't looking directly at him. "My whole life, I've fought against this feeling of not fitting in, and not being good enough. Growing up, before Mom died, I had this best friend back in

Washington. Everyone always looked at him first. When they found out he wasn't single, they looked at me second. I've always felt like I'm everyone's last resort. Not just sexually, but for any reason. No one asks me to go do things unless no one else is available. I'm not the guy who gets hit on in clubs. Unless everyone is drunk and their prospects are looking short, that is. I'm just not the cool kid. Theo says it's because I'm marriage material, which is probably one of the nicest things anyone has ever said to me. Because, really, I don't feel like I matter very much to this world. So I'm sorry if posing nude and stealing something for myself made you upset. That one thing is probably the only thing that's saved me for this long. So maybe don't make it about you. It's not."

For several minutes, Declan didn't respond. When he did, his choice of words surprised Ezra. "I can't say the same. Sleeping with everyone else was very much about you. I didn't think we would ever happen, and—more often than not—that drove me kind of crazy. Anytime I went out, I found myself gravitating toward anyone with your eye color, or their hair would be similar. Maybe the body type was the same. I kept trying to be satisfied with anyone else, but my heart always knew the difference. That's why I never slept with the same person twice. I know you can't help but to feel the way you feel. The thing is, though, you've always been my first choice. You've always been the only person I want."

"That's because you're weird," Ezra said, trying to lighten the mood. He didn't want to talk about anything heavy. One day, they would have to circle back to this, he was sure, but he just couldn't right now.

Declan flashed him a smile. "Nah. I'm just taller than everyone else. I can get a better picture of things than you can. There's no way I can miss the way you stand out. And you're wrong, by the way. You're no one's second choice. You're the intimidating choice. If people don't approach you first, it's because they need liquid courage, or they think they have zero chance with someone as hot as you are. It's nothing to do with you at all. If anything, you're too beautiful."

That sounded like bullshit to Ezra, but he appreciated it nonetheless. "I'll try to dial it down."

As they reached Declan's truck, Declan drew Ezra against his chest before unlocking and opening the door to hide them from view. He stared down into Ezra's eyes, stealing Ezra's soul with the love he couldn't hide. "I know it's asking a lot, but I don't want you to ever think about me with anyone else again, because it's never happening again. Like I said, back then, I didn't see any chance of us being together. You're mine now and I'm yours. No one exists for me but you."

That was fair. They hadn't been together back then. "Okay. Please don't be mad at me about those nude pictures."

Declan smiled. It was blinding. "I'm not. Those goddamn magazines got me through years of torture, thinking I couldn't have you. Maybe it took me some time to figure out what's best for me, but I'm not backing down now. I love you too much. I can't go back to living without you."

"Same." Even to Ezra's ears, his claim came out sounding breathless. He had never dreamed Declan would be here now, holding him and saying all the things he had said. Ezra would fight his way back to good health and find a way to make Declan happy if it was the last thing he ever did. He would never let Declan worry he had made the wrong choices. Ezra understood the chance Declan was taking on him. "You pick the mini-golf place and I'll pick dinner."

A smile exploded across Declan's face. "Deal."

"I love you, sexy protector."

Declan's smile slipped away and was replaced

with enough heat to blast Ezra off his feet. "I love you too, angel. I'll give you a beautiful life."

Ezra didn't doubt him. Not even for a second. They had silently loved each other too long. Neither of them could fail now. Losing each other wasn't an option left on the table any longer.

SIX

THREE WEEKS OF NONSTOP EATING, MAKING love, and pampering had Ezra feeling better than he had in a long time. No doubt that being back on his meds for three weeks also helped, but Ezra knew Declan made the biggest difference in his life. Without Declan, Ezra still would have tried to do better for himself, but he wouldn't have done half as well without Declan's constant presence. Declan did whatever it took to motivate Ezra. He nagged, demanded, and bribed Ezra back to health. Soon they would be home and would have to deal with something neither of them spoke about. The elephant in the room. Jessie.

Ezra lived in fear of what life would be like when they got home. There were too many unanswered questions. He didn't know if Declan planned to go back to work for Jessie and pretend they never happened. Ezra didn't know anything at all, and it was killing him. Every time he worked up the courage to ask, he felt like an idiot. Everything he thought to say sounded childish. Ezra had never known how to talk to Declan about them. That was something that hadn't really changed between them.

The drive back to California was made mostly in silence. Ezra swore he could feel the heaviness in the air. Declan toyed with Ezra's fingers while seeming lost in his own thoughts. Ezra wanted to climb inside his head and crawl through his every thought. He needed to know what would become of them when they weren't miles away from Jessie's wrath.

"I'm not broke," Declan said suddenly, startling Ezra from his internal panic.

He blinked at the odd statement. "Okay."

Declan didn't look away from the road. "I mean, I've worked for Jessie for seventeen years with barely any personal expenses. So I have some money saved. I mean, we might have to downsize some eventually, but I can take care of you."

As Declan's outburst sank in and finally made sense, a smile exploded across Ezra's face. "That's incredibly sweet, but why would you think you need to support us? I'm doing fine. We'll be good, baby."

Declan still looked worried. He shrugged. "I just think it's worth considering that Jessie might be angry enough to disown you. It's a given that he'll fire me before I can even say I'm quitting, but he won't likely be very happy with you either. We should get married before we tell him. He's a lot less likely to kill me if he knows that I'm not just toying with you."

Ezra's throat swelled. He wanted that, but not like this. Not coerced. Ezra wanted Declan to marry him because it was what Declan wanted. He tried to skate past the suggestion. "You are so sweet and amazing. But, first off, Jessie would never cut me off. No matter what I did. Secondly, I'm worth six point two million on my own without Jessie."

Declan glanced his way, looking horrified. "I'm sorry. What?"

Ezra covered his mouth, trying to fight back a smile. "YouTube, sweetie. All those videos I've been uploading for the past four years. Surely you didn't think I put that much work into it for nothing."

"People get paid to do that?" Declan sounded adorably outraged.

Ezra gave Declan's chest a pat. "Don't sound so

horrified. At least now you don't have to worry that we'll be poor."

Declan immediately turned cranky. "I was not worried about being poor. I didn't want you to be poor."

Declan went silent. Too quiet. It weighted the air. Ezra couldn't take it. "Are you mad at me now? I don't understand."

Declan flashed him a quick look. "No, baby. It's not that at all. I just... it's dumb. Never mind."

"Whatever it is, it's not dumb if it bothers you. Just say it. We've had too much time of not saying things."

With his gaze locked on the road, Declan's shoulder rose and fell in a half shrug. "It's just that you don't have any reason to marry me. Alleviating Jessie's anger was really the only play I had. Otherwise, I kind of fucked up any chance of you wanting to spend the rest of your life with me years ago. You already have everything you need. I'm not necessary in any way."

"Pull over."

Declan flashed him a worried look. "What?"

Ezra crossed his arms over his chest. "You heard me. Pull over."

Declan made his way to the shoulder of the road.

The minute they were safely parked, Ezra punched Declan in the arm. Declan didn't look fazed in any way. "What?"

"How dare you say you're not necessary? You're very necessary to me. Since the day Mom died, you've been the one who's been here for me. You're the one who made sure I ate and finished my online classes so I could graduate from high school. Jessie sure as heck wasn't volunteering to help with Calculus while he was high as an ivory tower. Then, there's Jessie. No one else in their right mind would've stayed by his side as long as you have. That matters to me. You have the patience of a saint and a heart as big as this truck. Declan, you are one thousand percent necessary to me. Don't you ever say you're not again."

"Okay."

Ezra huffed. "Is that it? Just okay."

Declan smiled. "Thank you and I love you."

With a shake of his head, Ezra looked away. "You're welcome and I love you too." He didn't want Declan to see his disappointment. Ezra wanted Declan to keep talking about marriage. Instead, he'd gotten an okay. What the fluff was that?

Declan leaned Ezra's way and pulled him in for a kiss. He didn't stop until Ezra was damn near climbing his body, breathless and hard. Then, with flushed cheeks and panting, Declan pressed his forehead to Ezra's. With his eyes closed, Declan took a deep breath, as if breathing him in. Ezra's heart twisted. He loved this man more than life. It didn't matter if Declan never talked to him about marriage again. They were enough for him. Ezra was happy with this life.

On the drive home, Declan thought everything through. He needed to talk to Jessie, but that wasn't his biggest and most immediate concern. Declan had other things to take care of right now. With the truck unloaded at Ezra's house, and a very happy Icarus tearing up Ezra's backyard, Declan hoped he could duck out for a few without being too missed.

"Can you do me a favor and go rest for a few while I run a couple of errands?"

Ezra's forehead furrowed. "Why do I need to rest while you're out?"

Declan hovered over Ezra and rubbed his arms. "For my peace of mind, please? You're still not at full bars and I'll worry if you're not resting."

"Sure. Is everything okay?"

"I have you. Everything is perfect. I just need to take care of some things and I know you'll try unpacking all these bags and whatnot while I'm gone if I don't ask you to sit down."

There was laughter in Ezra's eyes and Declan wanted more. Ezra stood on the tips of his toes and kissed Declan's chin. "Hurry back."

Declan claimed Ezra's mouth for a better kiss. It was hard to pull away. As much as Declan didn't want to leave, he also needed to do something important. "Remember. Relax. I'll be back as fast as possible." Ezra followed him to the door and closed it behind him. Declan's heart stayed behind as he climbed back behind the wheel of his truck.

Declan liked driving. It always gave him time to think. He made some of his best plans and decisions while stuck in traffic. Today was no different. The drive back from Arizona had given him plenty of time to work out a few plans. Now he needed traffic to be on his side because he had a few things to do. As if the universe was on his side, he got everything done in record time. He wondered if Ezra had actually done as he said or if he would find all their bags magically unpacked when he got home. As Declan climbed from the truck, he paused as he realized what he had just thought. This was his home now because Ezra was inside. That was his life. His steps picked up at the thought. He finally had the dream life he had wanted with every fiber of his being. Declan wouldn't take a second of it for granted.

He struggled a little with the back door while carrying two bags of food and drinks. After a minute, he managed. As he came through the door, Declan's heart stopped. Through the kitchen, he could see Ezra in the living room. He was on his side on the living room floor, looking like he had landed there in an unnatural position. Flashbacks of Ezra almost dying had Declan dropping the bags and running.

He skidded to a stop and dropped to his knees, only to find Ezra blinking at him in surprise like he was insane. "Hey, gorgeous. You got back fast."

"What are you doing on the floor? You scared the shit out of me." Declan might have roared the words like a complete lunatic, but he couldn't help it.

Ezra looked understandably confused by Declan screaming in his face. "I kicked back in the recliner, as you suggested, then your rotten dog came running in through the doggie door with a small animal of some kind in his mouth. When I screamed, he dropped it and it scurried under the couch. I locked him in the bathroom and was trying to figure out what it is and catch it."

Declan nearly collapsed in his relief. He wasn't sure if he would ever feel safe with Ezra being alone again. Declan dragged a deep breath in through his nose, trying to calm his racing heart. "So he's my rotten dog now, huh? I thought he was ours."

Ezra chuckled as he sat up. "He's yours when he's trying to eat small animals."

Declan pushed to his feet. "Okay. Let's see what it is. I'll lift the couch. You get ready to catch it." Ezra gave him a sharp nod. Declan lifted the couch. Ezra dove beneath.

"Awww. It's a baby bunny, Declan."

Declan dropped the couch when Ezra stood. He held a tiny brown ball of fluff against his chest. Declan eyed him. "He doesn't look any worse for the wear. Hopefully, Icarus was only trying to make a friend and not actually eat him. I'll get the back door and you can take him out." He watched as Ezra carried the bunny to the backyard, leaving him as far as possible away from the door. When Ezra turned back Declan's way, he was all smiles. Something in Declan's chest swelled. He thought it might be pride and happiness mixing together to choke him. Declan's hand automatically went to his pocket.

When Ezra was almost to the door, Declan dropped to one knee.

Ezra's steps faltered. "Are you okay?"

Declan held out the ring he had dug from his pocket. "Will you marry me?"

Ezra didn't even look at the ring. He launched himself into Declan's arms and wrapped himself around Declan's body. He kissed every place he could reach, making Declan laugh. "Are you kidding me? Yes. You didn't even have to ask."

Declan couldn't stop smiling at Ezra's over-the-top reaction. "Of course I had to ask." He pushed to his feet with Ezra clutched to his chest. "In truth, I actually had a much nicer proposal planned. I don't know what happened just then. You were walking toward me, and I couldn't wait a moment longer." Declan settled on the couch with Ezra in his lap. He took Ezra's hand and slipped the ring on his finger. It was a little loose, but he hoped Ezra would gain weight soon. Declan's throat tightened at the sight of the diamond on Ezra's finger. He started rambling to hide how moved he felt. "I stopped by that super fancy Italian restaurant you love and got your favorite dinner. I planned a nice dinner and thought about having candles, maybe followed by a bubble bath.

Something crazy romantic. Sorry I didn't make it longer."

Ezra snuggled close. He stared at the ring. "Are you joking? This was perfect. There's nothing more romantic to me than knowing you were so overcome that you dropped to one knee and asked me to marry you because you couldn't stop it from happening. This is beautiful."

Declan couldn't stop staring at Ezra. "You're beautiful."

A blush tinted Ezra's cheeks. A possessive roar sounded in Declan's head. Ezra belonged to him. He always had, but soon it would be official. No one would be allowed to touch Ezra but him. Declan shifted positions and lowered Ezra onto the couch. Ezra's expression transformed as he stared at Declan. Declan didn't doubt for a second he looked as hungry as he felt.

"I'm so in love with you." Even Declan heard the greedy growl to his voice.

"I'm in love with you too."

Declan gave Ezra a sharp nod, accepting his words as the truth. "You're mine. I don't want to wait a long time to get married."

A flush climbed Ezra's cheeks as Declan worked at the button and zipper on his jeans. "Okay."

While peeling off the lower half of Ezra's clothes, Declan kept up his end of the conversation. "You deserve a beautiful wedding, but I'm also impatient. How long do you need to plan a wedding? I don't know how long my patience will hold out."

Ezra openly fought to hold on to his thoughts as Declan kissed his bare knee. "Um. I don't know. Two weeks."

"I can give you two weeks." Declan held Ezra's stare as he kissed his inner thigh, working his way higher. "I'm about to suck your dick." Ezra whimpered. Declan wasn't done. "The sound of your pleasure better ring in my ears or I'll make you sorry."

Even turned on and at Declan's mercy, Ezra tried to be sassy. "Maybe I want to be punished. How will you make me sorry?"

"There are so many choices," Declan said, kissing Ezra's abdomen near his erection while being careful not to touch his cock. "I could just keep kissing here and here." He punctuated his words by kissing around Ezra's erection with no direct contact.

Another whimper fell from Ezra's lips. He squirmed beneath Declan's torture. "Please?"

At Ezra's plea, Declan lightly flicked his tongue across Ezra's crown. Just enough to drive him crazy.

An adorable growl vibrated from Ezra. An evil chuckle rose in Declan's throat. Ezra buried his fingers in Declan's hair and tugged, dragging him toward his hard cock. "Suck me."

That was what Declan wanted to hear. He sucked Ezra deep. His eyes fell closed as pre-cum coated his tongue. Declan's unhealthy obsession grew as he memorized Ezra's flavor. No one really knew the depth of Declan's insanity when it came to Ezra. He had loved Ezra in the dark. Declan had stalked and yearned. He had watched Ezra with something almost dark and brutal in his heart. Primal. It wasn't enough for him to be dating Ezra. Declan had to own him. Defile him. He had to keep Ezra for only himself. Forever.

Declan traced the lines of Ezra's body as he had while staring at his pictures in magazines. He touched Ezra in all the ways he had longed to do. Ezra whimpered and moaned while Declan licked and prodded. Every tug of Declan's hair and scratch at his skin was another memory seared into his brain, feeding his sickness. He was never fully satisfied until they were one. Lust had his skin tightening. He massaged his erection through his jeans as he swallowed Ezra's dick. An image of Ezra marrying him filled Declan's brain. He rubbed harder, his motions frenzied, sucking harder and faster. Ezra writhed. The images in Declan's head turned crazier by the second. In his head, they were chained together. Ezra couldn't get away. Declan did everything he wanted to Ezra while knowing they were together forever now. No one else would ever touch either of them again. They were all that existed for each other. Ezra was his. A cry tore from Declan's throat, muffled by Ezra's cock as an orgasm rocked him. Cum filled his underwear. Ezra pulled his hair hard as he cried Declan's name. Thick, salty fluid poured onto Declan's tongue. His eyes burned with unshed tears. He was more than in love with Ezra. Ezra was a sickness. Declan would cherish him for the rest of his days. Fuck anyone who thought he was crazed when it came to Ezra. He was. Declan was one hundred percent completely insane and it didn't matter at all. The subject of his imbalance had agreed to marry him. Nothing else mattered anymore. He was full.

SEVEN

THE DRIVE TO JESSIE'S WAS LIKE A TRIP TO Judgment Day. Declan knew the sooner they talked to Jessie, the better for everyone. Ezra spent several days a week visiting with Jessie and Declan wouldn't ask him to hide them. So he would be a man and talk to Jessie face to face. Plus, they were getting married sooner rather than later. That didn't give Declan much time. It was now or never.

Johnny met them in the driveway, prepared to sweep Ezra away. He was the one person Declan trusted to help him with this chore. Johnny opened Ezra's door. "Hey, Ez. It's good to see you." He hugged Ezra while Declan watched his hands, making sure he wouldn't have to break them. While Johnny had never showed in any interest in

106

anyone as far as Declan had seen, Declan wouldn't hesitate to unman him if he touched Ezra inappropriately.

Johnny moved to Declan's side with his hand extended. "Congrats, man. I don't know how things will go in there, but I'm happy for you two."

The way Declan's cheeks ached told the story about how big his smile had become. "Thank you. I appreciate your help with Ezra tonight. Things aren't likely to go well. It's best if Ezra gets his errands run while I hammer things out with Jessie."

Johnny's solemn expression said he understood the magnitude of Declan's situation. "You already have Theo on your side. That's more than half the battle."

Declan and Ezra exchanged a look. With a deep breath for courage, they headed for the back door together while Johnny stayed behind ready to whisk Ezra away. The door opened before they reached it.

"Yay. My brother is back and looking fantastic."

Ezra smiled and stepped into Jessie's outstretched arms. The instant their hug ended, Ezra headed for Theo and pulled him aside. They spoke in quiet tones. Theo checked out Ezra's engagement ring on the sly while Declan shook hands with Jessie.

"He looks good," Jessie said, sounding proud.

"Thank you. It looks like you've taken good care of him."

Declan fought a wince. Jessie would no doubt regret those words in a minute. "Yeah. He's doing great. The televisits with the counselor seem to be going well. He's taking his meds and eating. I'm proud of him."

Jessie nodded along. "I think the long trip was a good idea. Sometimes you just need out of your own space, you know?"

"Definitely." Declan's gaze slid Ezra and Theo's way. Theo gave Declan a pointed look and nod behind Jessie's back. Ezra moved to stand at Declan's side. They linked fingers. Declan took a deep breath. "There's something I need to talk to you about, Jessie."

Jessie's gaze moved from Ezra to Declan before dropping to their clasped hands and back to Declan's face. His smile slipped away. Declan could see Jessie putting the pieces together in his mind. His features hardened. "Uh huh." There was a definite threat to Jessie's tone.

"I've asked Ezra to marry me and he's accepted," Declan said—like ripping off a bandage.

Jessie's eyebrows rose. "This isn't April first, but I

damned sure better hear an April fools from one of you right now."

Declan felt sick. He didn't know what Jessie would do, especially after everything Wrecker had told him. "I've got boxes in the truck, so I can pack today."

Jessie ran his tongue over his teeth. Declan expected him to start swinging any second. "I brought you into my home. Around my baby brother."

"Jessie," Theo cut in, stopping him. "May I talk to you in the other room?"

Jessie glanced over his shoulder. "In a minute."

Theo took his hand. "Please?"

No one could miss how torn Jessie was in that moment. On one hand, he obviously wanted to kill Declan. On the other, Theo owned Jessie. Jessie couldn't deny him a thing. Jessie flashed Declan a cold look. "Don't move. This isn't over."

The moment they were gone, Ezra flashed him a huge grin. "Well, that was nowhere near as bad as I expected. Theo has a plan, so you should be good to start packing. Johnny is waiting."

Declan tugged Ezra into his arms and kissed his forehead. "Go. I'll be fine. If he kicks me out before you get back, I'll text you."

Ezra clutched the front of Declan's shirt—like he didn't want to pull away. "It'll be okay. You'll see."

"I love you." Declan wished there was some way he could express how much. This whole situation was choking him, but he couldn't lose Ezra. Not even for Jessie.

Ezra cupped Declan's face and drew him in. "I love you too. I promise you that Jessie will come around."

Declan swiped his lips across Ezra's. He believed in Ezra. Everything would be fine. They just needed to get through today. Ezra's kisses always fixed everything. He couldn't forget that now.

IT HAD BEEN A LONG TIME SINCE JOHNNY HAD been with him for the day. Back when Ezra still lived with Jessie, Declan always escorted him everywhere. Unless Jessie was on tour. Then Johnny had gone everywhere with Ezra. Johnny was the sweetest guy on the planet, and more times than Ezra could count, he had wished Johnny had been the bodyguard he fell in love with. If he had to choose one, that is. Obviously, now that everything had worked out with Declan, Ezra wouldn't even think about being with anyone else. But back then, life would have been so much easier if it had been Johnny. For one thing, Johnny was closer to Ezra in age. Johnny was twenty-seven to Ezra's twenty-four while Declan was thirty-four. Plus, Johnny was just uncomplicated. He was laidback and took everything in stride. Not to mention, Johnny was a really good-looking guy. His long blond hair had just a hint of wave to it. Back when Ezra had gone through his first battle with anorexia, Johnny would sit in the floor at Ezra's feet and let Ezra braid his hair. It had given him something mindless to do that really helped keep Ezra sane. On top of all those things, Ezra had never seen Johnny date anyone at all. As far as Ezra could tell, Johnny had never brought anyone home. He was a bit of a mystery to Ezra. In a lot of ways, that was a good thing.

Ezra poked Johnny in the arm as he drove. "So how are you liking being the head guard in charge with Declan gone?"

Johnny flashed him a sexy smile. His light brown eyes flashed with mischief. "Meh. Jessie doesn't go out that much anymore. Plus, Aspen got kind of lonely. Theo and Jessie stayed holed up in their cabin, so I was kind of stuck, finding things to keep me busy. They do have a cool bar there. It's called

Club Incubus. I spent *so* much time there. By the time I finally got to come home, they all knew my name."

The pressure in Ezra's chest eased just by talking to Johnny. "I'm sure Theo and Jessie enjoyed their time, though. While I was in Arizona, all my troubles seemed a world away."

"Jessie won't stay mad. He loves you too much, and whether he ever says it or not, he loves Declan too."

"Yeah. I'm not worried about Jessie."

Johnny tossed him a puzzled look. "What then?"

Even though Johnny was looking at the road and not him, Ezra shook his head. "It's just me, I guess. I don't want to fail at this, but it's only been three weeks since my hospital trip. It's possible I'm not strong enough to keep Declan happy while failing myself some days."

"Declan has been sickeningly in love with you for years. As long as you exist and love him back, you're set. He'll be happy with any version of you he can get any day of the week."

Ezra couldn't help but smile at the certainty in Johnny's every word. It felt nice to know other people noticed. Ezra hadn't only been dreaming that Declan loved him all these years. Some days, thinking Declan's love was all in his head, Ezra had thought he would go mad. But lately, everyone kept claiming they knew all along. Ezra felt free and vindicated.

The Back Porch came into view. Johnny snagged a parking spot close to the door. "Do you know, I've never been in this place," Johnny said, surprising Ezra. "I've been by here to pick you up and drop you off, or to bring Jessie by. But I've never been inside."

Ezra clapped his hands. He loved bringing sexy men inside The Back Porch. He felt like he was showcasing new wares for the patrons to enjoy. "Today is your lucky day, then. I can't wait to show you off."

A nervous-sounding laugh came from Johnny's side of the truck. "That doesn't sound ominous at all." Johnny slid from the truck and waited for Ezra so they could walk to the door together before saying anything else. "There are a lot of cars here for Wednesday night."

"There are a lot of cars here every night."

Johnny opened the door for him. "That's good. I like to see a small business thrive."

Ezra stepped inside and his feet froze. The lights were dimmed, and it was much louder than usual. A small stage had been set up in the back corner. "What the..."

Wrecker spotted him at the same time Ezra spotted Wrecker. They met halfway. "Ezra. You're back." He hauled Ezra in for a hug. "How are you feeling? I stopped by to see you. Did Declan tell you?"

"Yeah. Sorry. Things have been nuts. What's all this?" Ezra asked, motioning toward the stage.

Johnny spoke behind him. "Fuck, yeah. They have karaoke."

Wrecker's gaze slid Johnny's way and stuck. "Hi. Yeah. I've decided to start having different things—like karaoke—on Wednesday nights. The natives were getting restless around here. I'm Wrecker," Wrecker said, holding out his hand. "I own the place."

Johnny barely glanced Wrecker's way, but he briefly shook hands with him. "Johnny. I'm Ezra's bodyguard for the night."

That brought Wrecker's attention back Ezra's way. "Bodyguard? Why do you have a bodyguard?"

"He means babysitter," Ezra said, patting Johnny's stomach. "You can go play. Wrecker will watch me."

"Sweet," Johnny said, heading for the stage without looking back.

"What's going on?" Wrecker asked again, refusing to let it go.

Ezra shrugged. "Ah, you know, I fell out and had to be rushed to the hospital. So now Declan is refusing to let me do anything alone. I think I scared him a little."

"Declan? Why would Declan be the one deciding what you can and can't do alone? That guy is seriously worrying me."

A huge smile tugged at Ezra's lips at Wrecker's tone. He was the best kind of friend. Loyal to the bone. "It's fine. He's just looking out for me. Actually, we're getting married in two weeks."

"What in the..."

"That's why I stopped by. I know you're always busy, but I wanted to make sure you can make it," Ezra said, cutting him off.

"Make it to where? This is crazy sudden, and it's Declan." Wrecker sounded genuinely shocked.

"You know that it's not sudden at all. It's always been Declan and me, whether anyone admitted it or not. As to your other question, I'm still working on that. Or rather, Theo is. I want to have the wedding at Jessie's place, as long as Jessie isn't still trying to rip Declan's eyes out by then."

A stunning voice filled the air, making the entire building fall silent. As one, Wrecker and Ezra turned toward the stage. Johnny was at the microphone. He looked twice as hot with the multicolored stage lights highlighting his sharp features. He had a soulful sound with perfect pitch. His voice was beautiful. Ezra was floored.

"Goddamn." Wrecker's curse perfectly summed up the moment. Johnny had talent. Considering he worked for one of the world's most famous musical talents, Ezra didn't understand why he hadn't known that. Surely Jessie had heard Johnny sing at some point. Wrecker and Ezra stood side by side, equally stunned by Johnny. When the song ended, everyone flew to their feet to clap. With an awkward wave, Johnny kept his head down and jogged off the stage. He was back to Ezra's side in a flash.

"That was fun. I haven't sung in public in a long time."

"You're amazing." Even Ezra heard the awe in his voice. "Sing at my wedding. I'll pay you."

Johnny blushed, looking adorable. "You know you don't have to pay me, angel. We're friends."

They were friends, and—suddenly—the fears he

had confessed to Johnny on the drive over disappeared. He had fallen in a hole the past several months, and his brain had tricked him into thinking he was alone, but he wasn't. He had friends and family. They were closer than he had let himself believe.

"You should come by again the next time you're off," Wrecker said, pulling Ezra from his thoughts, only to realize he spoke to Johnny.

Ezra looked between them.

Johnny nodded. "For sure. I was telling Ezra I couldn't believe I've never been inside here before now. I can't count how many times I've driven him or Jessie over here."

"Well, now you know I'm here."

No one could miss Wrecker's emphasis on "I'm" in that sentence. Ezra hid a smile. Wrecker was definitely interested. Ezra decided to push a little. "Wrecker will be at the wedding."

"Oh, yeah. Definitely. Ezra is my favorite people. Wouldn't miss it."

Johnny eyed Wrecker from head to toe on the sly at the comment. "Maybe I'll see you there."

Ezra bit his lip to keep from smiling like an idiot. He was so happy and in love, Ezra wanted everyone to feel the way he did. "I guess we should get going.

Johnny still has to take me a few more places before the stores close."

Wrecker looked slightly disappointed. "Sure. Keep me posted. If you need some stuff catered, you know I'm your man."

"Oh shoot." Ezra rubbed his forehead. He had the hardest time keeping his thoughts together anymore. "I meant to ask you about that. It's super short notice, but there's absolutely no one I would rather have make our cake."

"Dang, darling. You know I'm all in. Whatever you need. I always have your back, even though it's Declan."

Ezra snorted. He knew it would take Wrecker a little time to warm up to Declan. "I love you."

Wrecker bent and kissed his cheek. "Back at you, babe. When you get a free minute, we'll figure out your cake. It'll be perfect."

With a final promise to call, Ezra headed back out with Johnny leading the way. Ezra tried not to worry about how things were going with Declan. He really hoped Jessie and Declan didn't kill each other before Ezra got back. He needed them to be okay. Otherwise, Declan was right to avoid Ezra for so long. Otherwise, Ezra had ruined Declan's life.

DECLAN PACKED UP HIS ROOM IN SILENCE AND tried not to think. Jessie was probably on the phone, hiring someone to kill him right now while Wrecker was telling Ezra how psychotic Declan was. Wrecker would be right, but still. Maybe Declan was a tad bit insane when it came to Ezra, but no one would ever love Ezra as much as Declan. To Declan's mind, that was the most important thing, but he couldn't keep Ezra from Wrecker's opinions forever.

Declan only had a few things left to pack. It had been two hours. Ezra and Johnny still weren't back. What if he didn't come back? A hint of panic had Declan's heart racing. What if Wrecker convinced Ezra to leave Declan?

"So, I've been paying you to sleep with my brother."

Declan's heart skipped a beat at Jessie's sudden appearance in the doorway. To hide his reaction, Declan snorted. He kept packing, avoiding Jessie's stare. "Only for the last few weeks. I'll pay you back, if you want. To be honest, I wasn't even thinking about the money. I've just been focused on Ezra's health."

"No. You were still taking care of him—like I

thought. It just seems you were taking way more care of him than I thought."

Declan took a breath and focused on Jessie. He looked surprisingly calm. "I have to say, you're taking this better than I expected."

A smile exploded across Jessie's face. "You can thank Theo for that. He tied me to the bed for a couple of hours. Then he made it really, really hard to think long enough to stay too mad."

"I'll bet he made it hard."

Jessie snorted at the innuendo. It turned into a chortle before he roared with laughter. Jessie swiped at his eyes. "Theo also took the time to make some points I might not have considered if left to myself to figure things out. You love Ezra. I think I've always known that. You two have always been closer than I wanted to admit. I know you wouldn't have risked our friendship if you didn't believe with everything you have that this is forever. So I have to think you love him as much as I love Theo. If you feel the same way about Ezra as I do Theo, then that's everything I've ever wanted for Ezra. I can't stand in the way of that."

"Thank you."

Jessie's smile hitched up a notch. "Just don't

forget that I can still afford to hire someone to break your kneecaps."

"I don't doubt it."

A pained look crossed Jessie's face. "After the shit Wrecker told me, I took your word over his, man. I trusted that Ezra was safe with you, even after everything that guy said. That's under my skin, though. I'm having a hard time letting that one go."

Declan couldn't call anyone a liar. "I know."

Jessie took a breath. "Tell me something, anything that'll make me go back to feeling the same about you, because—to be honest—I'm not sure you can be trusted anymore."

"I love him." Declan held Jessie's stare and prayed Jessie could see his soul. "You have nothing to fear from me. I just couldn't keep pretending that I could live without him. I know it doesn't make you feel any better about how things shook out, but Ezra will have the best and most faithful husband in the world. No one will treat him better."

Jessie's chest expanded on a deep breath. He rubbed the back of his neck—like he didn't know how to react. "Well, man. I guess I'm glad it's you, then." He pulled Declan in for a hug. "I've always thought of you as family, but it seems it'll be for real now." Emotions choked Declan as he hugged Jessie.

They would be family for real now. He hadn't truly thought of that before now. Declan also hadn't realized how much that meant to him. "So, when is this wedding?" Jessie asked, pulling away.

"I kind of wanted to talk to you about that," Ezra said from the doorway, pulling Declan's gaze his way.

"Hey, baby." Declan didn't know how long Ezra had been standing there, but he was overjoyed to see him. They hadn't been apart but a couple of hours. It was insane how much Declan needed Ezra to always be with him.

With a sweet smile in place, Ezra crossed the room and came to stand beneath Declan's arm—like he too didn't like being apart. Ezra focused on Jessie. "I was thinking, since you didn't get to have a big wedding and we're getting married, what if we have a double wedding? It doesn't have to be a huge affair. Neither of us needs that stress right now and you're my brother and I love you. Let's celebrate together."

Jessie had never been able to deny Ezra anything. It couldn't have been more obvious this was no different. "Obviously, I need to talk to Theo about it, but you know how much he loves you. I'm sure he'll be thrilled."

"Yay." There was no one alive who could resist Ezra's adorable smile.

Jessie cast a look around the room. "Well, it looks like you're almost finished. It'll be weird knowing you're no longer around." His face lit. "Maybe I can talk both of you into living here again. The place is big enough."

Ezra's laughter filled the room. "Nice try, but no. I know exactly how many men have slept in this room and I have no plans to join the ranks."

"I can find you a different room. Hell, we can build on to the house."

Ezra closed the distance between Jessie and him. "Let's save this chat for another day, okay?" He hugged Jessie. "Right now, you just got married and I'm about to do the same. Let's spend some time as newlyweds. Then we can see how we feel. You never know. This might be freeing. It's kitchen sex's time to shine. You might not ever want anyone to live with you again once you have the freedom of it being just Theo and you in the main house."

The way Jessie smiled at the idea of kitchen sex made Declan think they shouldn't eat here again. "All right." Jessie sounded disappointed but appeased. "I guess I'll let you two finish packing.

Promise me that you two will at least talk about my idea, though."

"I promise." Ezra sounded solemn—like he meant every word.

Jessie kissed Ezra's forehead. "That's all I can ask." He hugged Ezra again. A little too tightly, in Declan's opinion. Ezra's was still weakened, after all. "Ugh. I've missed you. Life needs to settle down so we can get back to having family nights."

Ezra patted Jessie's chest. "Everything will be back to normal before you know it. You'll see."

They exchanged a few more words and hugs before Jessie finally left them alone. Declan barely managed to hold his tongue until he was out of earshot. "What do you mean you know exactly how many men have slept in this room?"

Ezra shot him a pointed look. "Why did Jessie say he had taken your word over Wrecker's? And why did Wrecker want to know if you told me he stopped by when you didn't?"

"Touché." Declan would lose this argument no matter which way he went if he kept going, so he changed tactics. He invaded Ezra's space. "You know you're the only man who's ever slept in this room in my heart, right? It's always only been you."

Ezra rolled his eyes but didn't argue.

Declan didn't let up. "Tell me I'm wrong. How many times have you pictured my face and called my name while someone else fucked you?"

A blush tinted Ezra's face. He wouldn't meet Declan's stare. Yet he still clung to Declan's chest as Declan dragged him closer. "Stop. I get it."

Declan dropped his head and kissed Ezra's neck, seducing him. One of the things Declan found irresistible about Ezra was his innocence. No matter what they did, he couldn't be tainted. Ezra still blushed. He didn't cuss. He could pose nude a thousand times and Ezra would still be an angel in a world filled with demons. Ezra was beautiful. "It should finally be us; don't you think?" He kissed the shell of Ezra's ear. "In this room and under this roof, it should be us."

Ezra winced even as he held Declan tighter. "I think it is this room that's bugging me, though. It brings out the worst in me. When I left here on Christmas Eve, after you pushed me away for the last time, it was the final straw for me. This is the place where you broke me."

Declan's chest tightened. He couldn't look away from Ezra. Declan loved Ezra more than life. He couldn't let there be a single spot on the planet that reminded Ezra that Declan had ever rejected him.

"This is the place where you saved me," Declan admitted. "Come here." He took Ezra's hand and led him to a huge window by his bed. Declan positioned Ezra's body where he stood in the exact spot where Declan stood every night when Ezra still lived there. "If you stand here and look across the way, that's your bedroom window right there."

Ezra leaned closer to the window. "Oh, wow. It really is. I never realized our windows were angled like that."

Declan gave him a sharp nod. "I'm glad you didn't. Otherwise, I might not have gotten to watch over you the way I did." He took Ezra's hand again and led him to the bathroom. After flipping on the lights, Declan snagged Ezra's waist and sat him on the bathroom counter. Ezra's expression changed— like he knew exactly what Declan would say next as Declan moved to stand between his knees. "This is the spot where you stole my heart. We were positioned just like this. This wasn't the moment I realized I was in love with you. I realized I was in love with you when Lucifer died. This is the spot where I was standing when I fell in love with you."

Ezra's lips parted in surprise, obviously realizing exactly how long Declan had been in love with him. "I was sixteen. It was my first battle with the anorexia." Ezra glanced behind him at the mirror. "You made me look at myself in the mirror. Really look. Not at the parts of me that I hated, but at me. The person beneath the skin."

Declan couldn't look away from Ezra as he looked at himself. His throat swelled. He had loved Ezra so long and hard that—sometimes—he no longer knew if it was a healthy love. "Am I rushing you into marriage at the wrong time? Will you resent me later or will this be a setback for you?"

Ezra turned away from his reflection and met Declan's gaze. Instead of answering, he peeled off his shirt. He glanced over his shoulder again briefly before turning away from his image. "I still don't like what I see." The admission was a punch to Declan's heart, but Ezra didn't stop. "But you do." A whimsical-looking smile passed over Ezra's lips. "No matter how much I hate myself, you love me. I've always known that. We could wait until I'm completely recovered, if you want, but it won't matter. I loved you before I relapsed. You were all I loved, even at my worst. I'll still love you when I'm better. This disease isn't about you. You can't make it worse." Ezra cupped his face. "You do make me better, though. If you feel like we need to wait, we will. But that's not what I want and it's not what I feel like I need. No doctor has ever reached me at my lowest the way you do. I remember the night you made me look at myself in this mirror too. If asked, I could recite every word you said to me. Do you want to know what I saw when I looked in this mirror that night?"

Declan was mesmerized by Ezra. He needed Ezra's every thought. "What did you see?"

A beautiful smile touched Ezra's lips. "I caught the first real glimpse of what I've seen in my head every second since the first time we met. I saw us together." Ezra moved closer with each word he spoke until their lips met. Declan lost himself in their sweet kiss until it wasn't sweet any longer. Ezra tugged at Declan's shirt until Declan let him have it. Declan's body caught fire as Ezra massaged every place he could reach. He never tired of this feeling, being consumed. No one else had ever made Declan feel this way. He already knew no one else ever would. No matter what, they were in this life together. Nothing else mattered.

EZRA WANTED DECLAN INSIDE HIM. THAT WAS the only thing that would make things better. Declan had admitted to being in love with Ezra since he was sixteen. All these years that Ezra had longed and hurt while needing Declan, Declan had felt the same for every bit as long. They needed to be one person right now. Ezra didn't care about anything else.

"Please," Ezra begged when Declan didn't do more than kiss him. "I want to watch us together." Even he heard the desperation in his voice.

Declan dragged him from the counter and sat him on his feet. The intensity in Declan's eyes as he stripped Ezra was captivating. Once Ezra was nude, Declan kissed him sweetly before spinning him to face the mirror. As Ezra looked on, Declan led Ezra's hands to the counter. "Don't move."

At Declan's order, Ezra had to stiffen his knees. Declan dug through a nearby box, coming out with lube and a condom. Ezra watched the reflection of his every move. When cool lubed fingers toyed with his asshole, Ezra's gaze snapped to his image. His cheeks were flushed, and his lips were swollen from Declan's kisses. He didn't look like himself. For the first time, Ezra saw what Declan saw when he looked at Ezra. He couldn't look away as Declan kissed his shoulders and back. They were beautiful together because their love couldn't be missed. Suddenly, Ezra wanted the bed that should have always been his. This man belonged to him. Always had. It didn't matter if they married tomorrow, ten years from now, or if they had married back when Ezra turned eighteen. They had been chosen for each other by a higher power long before they were born. They were meant to be.

"Take me to bed."

Declan froze at the demand. His gaze met Ezra's in the mirror. "Are you sure?"

Ezra nodded. "That's my bed. Take me to bed."

Declan swept Ezra into his arms. His long stride ate up the floor between the bathroom and their destination. At the edge of the mattress, he climbed on without letting go of Ezra. He stared down at Ezra as he finally settled Ezra on the bed. Declan looked hungry—like he had been waiting a million years for this moment. He massaged Ezra's hip before moving on to his thigh. Declan urged Ezra's leg up and his knees apart as he settled between Ezra's thighs. Ezra's eyes burned from his refusal to blink.

"Tell me you love me."

"I love you," Ezra said without hesitation.

Declan's eyes fell closed, as if he savored the sound of Ezra's words. He surged forward and impaled Ezra with his cock. A gasp escaped Ezra. As always, they felt perfect and right. Declan lowered his head and captured Ezra's lips. His kiss was so sweet that Ezra found himself clinging to Declan, matching his pace. They were making love. It couldn't be mistaken for anything else. Even as pressure climbed his erection and tightened his balls, Ezra knew this moment was about way more than an orgasm. They were sealing a promise to each other. It was them against the world. Them against every battle—internal and external. As Ezra whimpered, cried, and shook in Declan's arms, he knew this was a forever love beyond a shadow of doubt. He didn't have to fight his battles alone anymore. It didn't matter if he was beautiful. They were. That was all Ezra needed to know to survive.

EIGHT

Singing at a backyard wedding hadn't been on Johnny's agenda two weeks ago. Now, here he was. It was funny. When he had moved to L.A. from Illinois eight years ago, he had big dreams. Johnny had ignored all the statistics. He had known all the way to his soul that he would be famous. Instead, he had immediately ended up living as a private security guard for one of the most famous drummers in history. The life he dreamed of having was within sight, except it wasn't his life. He kept someone else safe who had won the fantasy Johnny never would. As much as Johnny had accepted that he would never be the one on stage surrounded by fans, Johnny still couldn't help but dream again while singing at Jessie's wedding. After all, he had gotten to sing for famous people. That was pretty cool. Not everyone could say that.

Johnny had been so nervous leading up to his performance that he hadn't heard a word of the ceremony. Now that Ezra and Declan were married and Jessie and Theo had exchanged public vows, Johnny took in his surroundings with clearer eyes. Ezra had done an amazing job of throwing together a gorgeous outdoor wedding in a short time.

The food looked amazing. Of course, that was all Wrecker. Johnny's gaze slid Wrecker's way. He was a big dude. Rumor was he used to be a linebacker for a pro team. Now he owned a popular coffeehouse and baked cakes, apparently. The odd thing about Wrecker doing such a good job with the wedding was the hatred in his eyes every time he looked Declan's way. Johnny couldn't take the curiosity any longer.

Johnny carried a sleepy tux-wearing Icarus to Wrecker's side and filled the empty seat next to him. He followed Wrecker's gaze. The death stare he sent Declan's way couldn't be missed. "Does he owe you money or something?"

Wrecker startled, as if he had been so lost in his hatred that he hadn't known Johnny was there. A guilty-looking smile touched his lips. "Sorry. I know it's their big day and I should be happy for them..." He shrugged, as if he didn't know how to finish that statement.

"Should I worry you poisoned the cake?"

Wrecker flashed him an annoyed look. His lion-like eyes captured the sunlight, fascinating Johnny for a moment. He didn't know what it was about Wrecker. Johnny wasn't interested. He might work for and spend all his time with gay men, but Johnny was straight. He just liked Wrecker—like a friend. The color of his eyes was just cool or whatever. Johnny leaned away, putting a few more inches between them. He didn't want Wrecker getting the wrong idea.

"Ezra's my friend. I would never ruin his wedding."

Johnny shook his head. He forced his mind back on topic. "Then why are you eyeballing Declan like you're trying to decide where to stab him first? Do you have a thing for Ezra?"

A smile exploded across Wrecker's face, blanking Johnny's mind. "Naw, man. Ezra is like a little brother or something. I just worry about him. That's all. Declan isn't who I would've picked for him. He doesn't look at Ezra like he loves him. It's darker than that. I just worry." Once Wrecker started talking, it was like the floodgates opened. "I mean, I can't tell you how many times I've spotted him sitting outside Ezra's house late at night. I've also seen him sitting in the parking lot of my shop, watching Ezra. It's fucking weird. I feel like Ezra just married a crazy person."

Johnny couldn't stop smiling. It grew until he was full-on laughing

Wrecker's expression turned annoyed. "What? Why is this funny to you?"

Johnny swiped at his eyes. "I'm sorry. It's just that I've been Jessie's night guard for a long time. It's been illuminating. Would you like to know what I've seen?"

"Sure."

Johnny smiled at Wrecker's curt tone. "I've seen there's no pride in love," Johnny said, cutting right to the point. "Ezra stalks Declan every bit as hard as Declan stalks Ezra. Hell, they take turns at it. Declan leaves late at night to sit outside Ezra's place. Ezra drives by here a million times to see if Declan's at home. They're crazy for each other. It's long past the time they admitted it and put everyone out of their misery. If either of them ended up with anyone else, the world would've been less for it."

Wrecker looked thoughtful. "Huh. I have the

hardest time picturing Ezra pursuing anyone to that level. Before he told me he was marrying Declan, I've never seen him show an ounce of interest in anyone."

Johnny shrugged. "That's because it's always been Declan. Hell, the only reason he moved out at eighteen is because he couldn't stand watching Declan sleep around anymore. Declan couldn't settle down because he felt wrong for wanting the only person he cared to settle down with. They're just in love, man. It's made them crazy."

Wrecker went back to watching Declan. The hatred was gone from his eyes now. He nodded, looking thoughtful as his gaze swung back Johnny's way. "May I buy you a drink from the complimentary bar?" Wrecker's smile had Johnny's gaze dropping to Wrecker's lips.

"I'm sorry if I've given you the wrong impression. I'm straight."

Wrecker's smile grew, making Johnny realize he still stared at Wrecker's mouth. "Dude, it's a beer. Not a marriage proposal. Maybe it's been a while since I had a straight friend, but—from what I remember—y'all drink too."

A snort escaped Johnny. He tried shaking off

whatever spell Wrecker weaved over him. "Of course. Sorry. I don't know what I was thinking."

Wrecker slapped him across the back and stood. "You thought I was hitting on you. It's cool, though. Maybe I was or maybe I wasn't. I guess you'll never know. Let's get a drink."

Johnny took a breath and stood. He didn't know what had gotten into him, but he would make it stop. Since moving to L.A., Johnny hadn't made a lot of friends. Wrecker seemed like a cool guy. They could hang out, if Johnny would stop being dumb. Weddings always messed with him a little. That was all. There was nothing for him to worry about. Nothing at all.

As Declan drew Ezra back against his chest, Ezra's smile grew. He hadn't thought he could smile any harder today. Declan's lips skimmed the shell of his ear. Ezra's eyes fell closed at the sensation.

"I definitely have the greatest husband here."

Ezra covered his mouth, trying to control his out-of-control grin at Declan's claim. "How would you know? I've only been your husband for like an hour."

"I didn't need that long to know no one else could make me happier. I already knew that."

An idea struck Ezra. "Hey. Do you think anyone would notice if we disappeared?"

Declan chuckled. The sound vibrated against Ezra's skin, making him bite back a happy sigh. "Yes. People would notice. We still have to cut the cake. Wrecker already hates me. Imagine what he'll think if I reject his fucking cake."

Devilry rose inside Ezra and wouldn't let him go. "We should let Jessie and Theo do the cake cutting and slip away. Wrecker is hanging out with Johnny. He won't even notice we're gone."

"Um. No. You're not leaving me the center of attention. This was your idea," Theo said, appearing beside them. "I was already happily married. I didn't need a wedding."

Ezra openly pouted. "Oh, come on. You deserve to be the center of attention. Let everyone take your picture and plaster it on every tabloid. Do you have any idea how many people will be pestering you for interviews and praising you for getting Jessie clean?"

Theo's light blue eyes slid Ezra's way. He didn't look amused. "Uh, yeah. They're already calling all hours of the day." Declan squeezed Ezra tighter and placed several loud kisses on his temple. Theo looked between them. "Fuck. You two really are about to disappear on me, aren't you?"

Declan took Ezra's hand. "Nope. This is a rockstar's wedding. If my baby wants a swift exit. Let's make it a metal one." Declan headed for the table where the cake sat waiting, and Jessie hid from everyone drinking. He looked the part of the rockstar —top hat and all black.

As Ezra looked on in horror, Declan met Jessie's stare and grabbed a handful of cake. A huge and evil-looking grin spread across Jessie's face as he did the same. Ezra didn't have time to react before he found the delicious dessert crushed in his face. He tried licking away what he could. Ezra heard Theo yelling and laughing as Ezra dove for the table. A mad scramble went down as everyone tried grabbing for a piece, ruining Wrecker's creation. Declan was too tall for Ezra to get even, so instead, he smeared a piece of cake across Declan's crotch. Declan yanked him off his feet and unabashedly licked icing from Ezra's face while Ezra fought to get away.

Theo and Jessie fought the same battle. Their dark tuxes were smattered with white icing. When Theo finally managed to get even with Jessie, Jessie grabbed Theo around the middle and dove for the pool. Loud peals of laughter rent the air before the water swallowed the sound. They came up kissing. It was such an intense display that Ezra turned his head. His gaze collided with Declan's. Declan's evil smile was all the warning he got before he too was sinking in the pool. All was forgiven when Declan rescued him. Their lips met as they surfaced. Laughter circled them as more people cannonballed into the pool. But the world slipped away for Ezra in Declan's arms. All he knew was love and peace, even while surrounded by chaos, which pretty much summed up Ezra's life. Only when he was in Declan's arms did Ezra feel steady and complete. Now they were officially forever. Until death do they part, and beyond. That sounded damn good to Ezra.

KEEP AN EYE OUT FOR THE NEXT CANDIED Crush, *Beautifully Wrecked*.

Please consider leaving a review at the retailer where this book was published. Reviews really help with a book's visibility, which ensures I can continue writing. Thank you, Charity.

ABOUT THE AUTHOR

Charity Parkerson is an award winning and multi-published author with several companies. Born with no filter from her brain to her mouth, she decided to take this odd quirk and insert it in her characters.

*Eight-time Readers' Favorite Award Winner

*2015 Passionate Plume Award Finalist

*2013 Reviewers' Choice Award Winner

*2012 ARRA Finalist for Favorite Paranormal Romance

*Five-time winner of The Mistress of the Darkpath

Connect with her online:

—Sign up for my newsletter: http://bit.ly/CharityNews

—Join my readers' group on Facebook: http://bit.ly/CharitysTribe

—Website: charityparkerson.com

—Facebook:
facebook.com/authorCharityParkerson
facebook.com/TheMenofSin
—Twitter: twitter.com/CharityParkerso
—Instagram: Instagram.com/sinnerauthor